THE AGE OF DISCOVERY
AND OTHER STORIES

THE JOURNAL NON/FICTION PRIZE

The Age of Discovery

and other stories

BECKY HAGENSTON

MAD CREEK BOOKS, AN IMPRINT OF
THE OHIO STATE UNIVERSITY PRESS
COLUMBUS

Library of Congress Cataloging-in-Publication Data
Names: Hagenston, Becky, 1967– author.
Title: The age of discovery and other stories / Becky Hagenston.
Description: Columbus : Mad Creek Books, an imprint of The Ohio State
    University Press, [2021] I Summary: "The real and the fantastic collide in
    stories that span from Mississippi to Europe and from the recent past to
    the near future"—Provided by publisher.
Identifiers: LCCN 2020055604 I ISBN 9780814257944 (paperback) I
    ISBN 0814257941 (paperback) I ISBN 9780814281260 (ebook) I ISBN
    0814281265 (ebook)
Subjects: LCSH: Short stories, American—21st century.
Classification: LCC PS3558.A32316 A73 2021 I DDC 813/.54—dc23
LC record available at https://lccn.loc.gov/2020055604

Cover design by Susan Zucker
Text design by Juliet Williams
Type set in Palatino Linotype

Contents

Perishables / 1

Witnesses / 15

Seven Ravens / 29

The Age of Discovery / 41

The Celebrity / 55

Young Susan / 59

Hi Ho Cherry-O / 67

Sea Ice / 77

Sharon by the Seashore / 95

Cornfield, Cornfield, Cornfield / 101

Rise / 103

Hematite, Apatite / 113

Fillies / 127

Basic Commands / 133

The Sitters / 149

Starry Night / 155

In the Museum of Tense Moments / 171

Storage and Retrieval / 177

Acknowledgments / 187

Perishables

Dean and Gina from across the street are the first to arrive in the grassy island in the middle of the cul-de-sac. Gina is hauling two folding chairs and Dean pushes a portable grill that looks like a robot trying to fly. I watch from my living room window as they stake their territory. Dean used to be a history professor. He would take students to European battlefields every summer and then submit fraudulent receipts to the study abroad office. I know this because I used to be the study abroad director, and when I asked about the receipts, he said something about an affair with a woman in Normandy. Something about never doing it again, even though he did it again. They seem cheerful, Gina and Dean—well-adapted to life off-line. "Ignorance is bliss," Dean actually said to me the other day, and I said, "Until we're rounded up and shot," and he scowled.

"Dad." My daughter Lorna is standing in the middle of the room wearing the pink shorts and halter top her mother bought last year for her fifteenth birthday. This is apparently a "fun outfit," so I've refrained from saying she looks ridiculous. "I'm not eating a dead deer." She puts her fingers on the window, leaving smudges; in the other hand, she's clutching her iPhone, which hasn't worked in months. Outside, Tom Reardon is pulling a deer carcass on a red wagon, his shotgun slung over one shoulder. "Plus, all we have to bring is canned shit like *beans*. Goddamn it. Where can we get corn chips?"

I don't bother scolding her for language or reminding her how lucky we are that we still have so much canned shit. "First," I say, "build a time machine." This is our joke, whenever we realize we're out of something we never realized we loved so much: Gatorade, contact lens fluid, Altoids, toilet paper, corn chips. There are other things, I know, that Lorna misses and doesn't tell me about. And there actually had been corn chips until a week ago, when I scavenged them from the back of the cabinet in the middle of the night. I went outside and ate the entire bag myself, staring up at the amazing sky. Electricity is sporadic now, maybe two hours a day. The stars are so bright, and there are so many of them. I stared into the Milky Way as I self-ishly crunched, feeling like a terrible person for denying my daughter her corn chips, yet unable to stop. Then I threw the empty bag over the fence to where the Morgans used to live, before—according to rumor—they left for the Alabama border. All four of them: first the teenage boy and girl, then the parents.

"What if we already did build a time machine, and this is where we ended up anyway?" Lorna asks. She looks worried, as if this is an actual possibility.

"Look on the bright side," I say. "This will go down in history as the most disastrous block party of all time."

"In all of human history," Lorna agrees.

"I'll tweet about how awful it is. As if summer in Missis-sippi doesn't already suck, now it sucks even more."

"I'll post on Facebook how much it sucks."

"I'll post Instantgrams—was that it? I'm starting to forget."

Lorna shrugs. She stares down at the dead phone.

I try again: "I'll text you if I get stuck in any awkward conversations."

"Okay." She looks up. Her hair is too long and hangs in her eyes and makes her look like her mother did at her age. "I'll come to the rescue, I guess."

"And then Mittens will show up, and we'll be like, wait. This isn't *so* bad."

Lorna stares at her phone again. "Let's not talk about Mittens."

"No," I say. "Let's not."

•

It was Joe and Marcie Dobbs' idea to have the block party. They live two houses down, an African American couple with grown children who used to arrive for summer visits in Subarus with California license plates. Joe is tall and bald, a former cop, and when I saw him standing on my doorstep last week, I thought: *Shit, he knows about the notes.* But he was smiling in a way that suggested he didn't, so I pulled open the door.

"Why, hey there, Matt," he said. "How's it going?"

I told him it's going fine, considering, and he nodded as if this was profound information. "Is your girl still here?"

"Lorna," I said. "Yeah, she's here. Her mother's still in Boston."

He opened his mouth, then seemed to decide against whatever he was going to say. I considered asking after his own probably-dead family in California, but instead I said, "What's up, Joe?"

And he told me that he and Marcie were organizing a party for Saturday, for everybody who was left on our block. "Just a time to relax and fellowship with each other. Grill up some veggies, eat some perishables before they go to waste. Tom Reardon's going to shoot the deer that keeps eating his greens."

I don't like it when people use *fellowship* as a verb. But I said, "Sounds good, Joe. Thanks for the invite. We'll be there Saturday." It was a moment later that I realized I didn't know what day it was and hadn't known for weeks.

•

These are the people left on our block: Dean and Gina, Joe and Marcie, Wayne Jenkins and his son Josh, and Tom Reardon—who is about my age, but is as different from me as it's possible to be. Beard, big white pickup truck with NRA and Confederate bumper stickers. We occasionally exchange tense words about whose turn it is to mow the island. His wife—according to Wayne Jenkins—left him a few years back. "Can you blame her?" Wayne said, and we both chuckled. This was before Wayne's son, Josh, broke my daughter's heart. Josh is seventeen, moon-faced, both thin and soft. A boy who wears visors inside. A boy who, last year, put a big sign in the middle of the island inviting the Morgan girl to the junior prom. She accepted, apparently: I remember seeing the two of them walking hand in hand a few times. According to Lorna, Melissa Morgan is (was?) a slut and a psycho, and Josh never loved her and only dated her because he felt sorry for her. When she and her family left for the Alabama border, Josh was glad.

"Okay, that's interesting," was all I could think to say.

MM would rather die than date Josh Jenkins!! Maybe she'll get her wish!!!

That was the note I wrote, folded into a neat football-tri-angle, and launched across the street into the yard of a seventy-year-old man named Bill with a Prayer is America's Only Hope sign in front of his house. Earlier, I'd written this note—*If Prayer is America's Only Hope, we are fucked*—and launched it into the Jenkins' yard.

I found this immensely satisfying, almost as satisfying as posting anonymous comments on blogs and right-wing websites. Almost as satisfying as being awake at one, two, three in the morning, engaging in word warfare on my computer while my wife Renee slept in the other room. But then, of course, she walked in on me while I was telling some complete stranger that he (or she) was too stupid to live, *so go ahead and throw yourself in front of a train, you goddamn piece of shit.*

"What are you *doing?*" Renee murmured behind me. "Good God. Who do you hate so much?"

"I have no idea," I admitted, and she started to cry.

•

"That smells good," Marcie is saying when I make my way out to the island with my bowl of cold baked beans. She's referring either to the yellow squash on the grill or to the smoldering venison in a make-shift fire pit. I put the beans on a card table next to a pile of tomatoes and cucumbers. Tom is relaxed cross-legged in a folding chair, flanked by citronella tiki torches, his shotgun atop his lap. He looks like a hillbilly on a front porch with his self-righteous smile. *Fellowshipping.* His smile dims a little when he sees me.

"Looks like somebody didn't get around to mowing, am I right?" he says, and pulls a cigarette from his front pocket.

"Well, I guess I was thinking it was Bill's turn," I lie. Bill disappeared a couple weeks ago. So, oddly enough, did his Prayer sign. He left his house unlocked, a note on the kitchen table: *Please take everything. God Bless.* But—as I saw for myself—there was nothing really to take. No bottled water, no canned goods. Just a useless TV, a cat-clawed sofa.

"Bill's turn is over," says Tom, and something about the way he says it makes me wonder if he's the one who took all the canned goods.

"Good to see you, Tom," I say, as if this is just a regular block party and he's just a regular asshole. I turn toward the sound of Wayne and Josh's jubilant voices carrying over the lawns, along with what sounds like eighties pop music.

"Anybody call for entertainment?" Wayne says, and this is apparently Josh's cue to heft an ancient battery-powered boom box above his head, like a love-sick kid in a teen movie. I don't think either Josh or Lorna has seen this movie, but I see him turn to look at her shadow in the living room window; I can feel the weight of her eyes as she stares out. Then she's gone, a ghost vanishing. I see Josh's face flush. Paula Abdul is begging someone to love her forever, and it now seems less like a frothy pop song than a challenge, or a dare, or a command.

•

Lorna hasn't left the house in weeks. "There's gunshots outside," she told me last week, and I told her she was wrong. "Or yes, there's gunshots," I amended. "But it's people hunting rabbits and squirrels. It's not Mittens."

"Shut up about stupid fucking Mittens," she said.

I tell myself I'm being a very good parent, in light of the circumstances. In Boston, Lorna was starting to get in with what Renee called "a bad crowd," meaning kids who skipped school and drank. I reminded Renee that *we* were the bad crowd, once upon a time. I reminded her of those nights I drove us around drunk in my mom's Rabbit, the time we drove stoned to Foxborough in a snowstorm.

I didn't remind her of what I have come to think of as my "rotten years," after my ten-year-old brother died. I was twelve. She didn't know me then, when I punched a kid for saying Timothy killed himself. She didn't know me when I put rotten eggs in mailboxes, sent death threats to classmates. A day on Lake Winnipesaukee, Timmy and I set out in a rowboat. A storm swept in. I saved myself but couldn't save my brother. So I became the kid who sent threatening letters to the principal, signed with the names of other students, kids who used to be my friends. I was the boy whose family had to move from New Hampshire to Massachusetts to get away from the rumors and from my own dark heart.

Renee and I split up three years ago. We congratulated ourselves on our impressive run—almost thirty years as a couple—and then I applied for jobs and ended up here. I went to Boston every Christmas, and Lorna came to visit me for a month every summer. I thought of dating again, then thought better of it. And at some point, Lorna and Josh started "hanging out," as she called it. I'm not sure what happened between the two of them, but it happened— whatever it was—when I was still biking to the university to try to pretend everything was normal. Even though summer school was cancelled; even though the internet was out, and the IT team—who I feel extremely sorry for—had abandoned their offices. "Did he hurt you?" I asked when I found her crying at the kitchen table, writing FUCK YOU, JOSH over and over on a piece of notebook paper. "Did he *kiss* you?" And she got up from the table and slammed into her room.

That's when I began to feel the itch again. I hadn't trolled for almost a year, but now I wanted to tell the entire world to fuck off—starting with Josh and with Bill and his Prayer sign. When I'd told Bill what I did for a living, he'd said, "I would not care to go abroad. Too many *Moslems*."

So I launched the note meant for Bill into the Jenkins' yard, and the note meant for them into his. It seemed safer that way. But I had too much to say. I started filling a cardboard box with notes, folded in tiny squares, and hid the box in my closet. Mostly, the notes I write are just plain immature. *God is an Ass Clown. You are all religious nut-jobs. You're too stupid to know how stupid you are.* Really dumb stuff. *Get back in your redneck pickup truck and drive off a cliff, you moron.*

Statistics show that most guns are used on their owners. Here's hoping.

I am not this person, I tell myself in the middle of the night, as I write, *Are you too stupid to know your husband is fucking a woman in Normandy, or are you too smart to care?*

My heart pounds. *One more,* I think. *One more.* The box is almost full. I used to crave the thrill of someone writing back, horrified, calling me an evil, vile human being. Now, nobody writes back, and the box gets fuller. I have suggested that children are better off now that they won't have to go to school. I have said that Christians are fools, that Southerners are ignorant. But I'm a good person, I tell myself. This isn't hurting anyone.

•

Tom Reardon is staring at the boom box like he wants to shoot it. I have some old Johnny Cash tapes somewhere. The thought briefly occurs to me that I could get them and put an end to Paula Abdul, but I decide against it. Gina and Dean have started grooving next to the grill. Somehow, there's beer, and Wayne hands me a bottle of warm Michelob.

Lorna has appeared in the yard, holding her phone in both hands. She seems stunned to find herself outside, blinking like a sleepwalker. I see Josh swivel in her direction.

"Hey, there," I call to her, but she doesn't answer, just heads around the side of the house, probably to pick some wild strawberries. Josh watches her go.

Wayne has started talking about the rumors. Gina sidles up, chewing on a carrot. Then Joe and Marcie. Tom, Dean. We're all standing in a circle on the grassy island as if it's a life raft about to sink.

We'll be completely out of water by next week, Wayne says. Electricity—which we have sporadically now—will be gone. And has everyone noticed the way the animals keep disappearing? The dogs have run off. Even the squirrels: aren't there fewer of those? There have been explosions near Columbus, Mississippi. An entire eleventh grade class was seen marching down Highway 82, waving black flags. Or were they American flags? The university burned. Churches are locking people out—or in. Which is it?

Before the internet blackout, we watched footage of helicopters burning, troops marching—but whose helicopters and whose troops? There used to be a news reporter who came around on horseback. He was blonde and wore a pink tie. This is how we found out about Mittens at the Alabama border. Or was it the Tennessee border? Or was it our own government, come to rescue us? Then came the looting. The sound of gunshots in the night. Fliers appeared in mailboxes, a simple message: YOU CAN MAKE A DIFFERENCE IF YOU JOIN US! And people began to disappear.

"Damn," says Dean. "I never thought I'd say this, but I wish I had a gun."

Dean: at least he's studied battlefields. Even without a gun, he knows more than I do about how to stay alive in a war. Strategy. What can I offer? I can show you Oscar Wilde's tomb at Père Lachaise; I can tell you the entry fee to the British Museum. I can tell you about my honeymoon in Venice with my twenty-year-old wife, how we dared each other to jump in the Grand Canal. How it all seemed so dangerous.

•

When I first moved here, I was braced for everything I'd heard about Mississippi: the racists, the ignoramuses, the disregard for common sense and healthy eating habits. I fended off a few offers to attend church, and maybe a few people smirked at my hybrid car. When I told Bill across the street—after about three inquiries about my "home church" and my marital status—that I was a divorced atheist, he didn't gasp and scream hellfire; he just patted my arm and said, very sadly, "I will pray for you."

Even Tom Reardon helped me tear down a rotten doghouse in the back yard when I first moved in. Gina and Dean had me over for drinks, and we talked about the best bars in Brussels. My colleagues at the university welcomed me. Everyone has been kind. Which is why I feel even more awful about the things I think and feel and write on tiny pieces of paper.

Lately, I've directed some comments to myself: *What is wrong with you?*

You are a terrible father.

How can you protect your child when you don't believe in any of the things you need to believe in?

"We're safest if we stay put," Joe is saying.

You are a vile vile person.

"I've got a shotgun you can have," Tom tells Dean. He nods in my direction. "You, too."

I don't bother telling him I've never fired a gun in my life. I say, "Thank you," because I am grateful.

"We could pray every day, make our own church," says Gina. Nodding heads.

Really, the only person I hate right now is Josh, with his goofy smile and his backwards baseball cap. This is a terrible thing to admit, but I wish he would just leave. Disappear. He pops out Paula Abdul, pops in Wham!. These cassettes must be his father's or his grandfather's. Or his mother's. What happened to his mother? I realize I don't know.

"Anybody want another grilled squash?" Dean says. The fire is dying down. The baked beans are gone. Wayne is eating from a box of stale Wheaties. I discovered the other day that I have wild wheat growing in my yard. Could I make bread? Yes, I decide. We can survive this, until some switch flips the world back on again.

I think of overhearing Lorna a few weeks ago, talking in her room. "Yes," she was saying. "He's fine. He's very nice." Long pause. "No, of course not! Geez." A longer pause. "He says it's all in the Bible anyway, nothing to be afraid of."

I rapped on her bedroom door.

"What!" she shouted.

"Who are you talking to, honey? Who are you talking to about the Bible?"

She opened the door, held up her dead phone. Her eyes were bright. "I'm talking to Mom," she said. "Are you happy?" And then she slammed the door in my face.

Fine, I thought. *Do what you have to do.* If she wants to believe in an imaginary person looking out for her, that's fine. Maybe it's good.

"We can boil the water from that pond behind the development," Marcie is saying.

"My generator'll work for a few months," says Wayne.

The cassette tape clicks itself off mid-song, and no one flips it. The locusts and the crickets are a riot of sound. The sun is gone; the street is dark, and the mosquitos are out in full force, despite the citronella torches. I can see the whirl of galaxies above, a small fire far away. A bonfire, perhaps. Another block party. Or something else.

"Let's not call them invaders or beheaders," I suggested a couple months ago to Lorna.

"What then?"

"Something less scary. The least scary thing you can think of."

"Like Mittens?" She laughed. We once had a cat named Mittens, a white rollie-poly kitten who grew fat and lazy. She'd curl up at your neck while you slept.

"That's it. There's no reason to be afraid of Mittens."

She laughed again, then grew sober. "Mittens got hit by a car."

"Let's bow our heads," says Joe now.

I bow my head, close my eyes, and try not to think of the study abroad students who were in the air when whatever happened happened. I try not to think of the students deep in the Paris metro when everything stopped. "Have faith," is what people say. Believe in what you can't know for sure.

The fire in the pit is flittering out, everyone fading to shadow. The beer—my first in months—has made me feel calm, benevolent, even hopeful. Inspired.

"I'll be right back," I say, and I dash into the house, into my dark bedroom, and pull the box of notes from the closet. I'll burn them, burn the whole box. *See?* I will say. *I have something to offer after all.*

"Kindling!" I call, as I carry the box out to the island, to the sputtering fire. The dark sky is growing darker; there's a smell of rain in the air.

Joe is still standing in the middle of the island, tiki torches burning around him like in the old TV show that Renee and I used to watch. "Whatever our differences, wherever we come from." Joe looks at me. "We have the greatest chance of survival if we're in this together." Yes—*Survivor*. That was it. I feel myself grinning, even though I know nothing is funny. "We can't have any more of our people, especially our young people, running off to the border."

Josh and Lorna are shadows in the bushes, but I can tell they're holding hands.

It's them, I realize, and my heart feels like a grenade, the pin in Lorna's hand as she moves away, into the darkness. They're the young people planning to run off. And here I was worried about him kissing her and breaking her heart. Now I remember something else I heard her saying on the phone to her imaginary Mom: *It's all going to be okay if we stay on the right path. We can make a difference!*

She never fucking talked like that before.

The fire is almost out. I squat next to the fire pit with the box, scoop a handful of paper into the dying flames. There's a spark, a flicker of new flame. A gunshot in the distance. I add more paper, create more light, stand and scan the yard for my daughter. "Lorna!"

I feel a sudden gust of wind, and then the notes are in the air, some still folded, some on fire, some falling like sparks, some rising like snow.

"Fortune cookies!" says Marcie, chasing a piece of paper into the street.

"Lorna?" I call, and I head across my lawn, but even in the firelight I can't see where she's gone. Another gust of wind whiffles the shrubs; a piece of paper drifts by my face.

First, I think, *build a time machine.*

Everyone is laughing, even Tom, as the notes fly and burn and flutter, as if I've brought them party favors, a reason to celebrate. I make my way around the house, past the sweet-smelling jasmine bushes and wild strawberries, all the way back to the island and its torches and fire. "Lorna!" I shout. But she doesn't answer. The stars wheel above me, and the laughter of my neighbors trails into silence as they catch hold of those falling scraps of paper—no one's fortune but mine—and unfold them, and begin to read.

Witnesses

It had been a long, annoying four days and now they were arguing in the taxi. Carrie had brought up Ellen's arrest last year, so Ellen called Carrie a fool for marrying a man she hardly knew: no wonder they'd divorced after six months! And who had invited Ellen to France anyway, Carrie wanted to know, because she was pretty sure she'd invited herself. Now, as the taxi darted down the boulevard toward the Nice airport, Ellen was about to say something deliberately ominous to her sister, but in a joking sort of way—*Fingers crossed for a plane crash so I don't have to suffer through your company much longer!*—when the windshield shattered and the taxi driver slammed on the brakes. Their luggage tumbled in the trunk; Ellen lurched forward and smacked her forehead against the seat in front of her. When she sat up, the taxi driver was already in the street shouting. Traffic was stopped all around them.

"What happened?" Ellen said, pointing to the windshield.

"Come on," Carrie said, and then she was pulling Ellen out of the taxi.

"What *happened?*" Ellen said again. "Did we hit someone?" But her sister was yelling—of course everyone spoke French but Ellen—and the taxi driver was flinging the trunk open, and people were running up from the beach. Ellen was drunk; she had heat stroke most likely, she was sunburned, she had come to France with the sister she'd barely seen in half a decade, who was now shouting: *Grab your suitcase, follow me, come this way, hurry, we can find another taxi and still catch our flight.* Carrie was pulling her big blue suitcase by the strap, both of their backpacks hung from her shoulders.

Ellen wasn't hurrying. She had her phone out, and she was filming the shouting taxi driver, the blue sky, the blood, a woman's black sandal, Carrie turning to yell, "What the hell are you doing?"

"But we're witnesses!" Ellen cried, jogging after her sister, already appalled and ashamed of herself. It wasn't as if she or Carrie had medical training! What could they have done? Nothing, she told herself, making excuses in her head, repeating, *We were witnesses. We were.*

•

One hour before her death, Mary floats. It's such an ordeal getting into and out of the sea—so many slippery stones!— that once you're in, you might as well stay a while. She's not the best swimmer in the world, but luckily you don't have to be. She floats on her back and watches the planes coming in over the water. Turn the other way and there are the hotels: the Westminster, the West End, the Negresco with its pink dome. And what a view on the beach: leathery old men in high-waisted Speedos, good for them. Topless women, breasts brown and sagging. Mary considered letting her own forty-five-year-old boobs float free, but it's perfectly okay, she has decided, not to do this. Maybe when she's home in Maryland she'll tell the other secretaries in the art department that she did; she might tell her husband, Henri, if he's still talking to her.

"The fabulous Frenchman," her friends like to call him. "The international man of mystery." Ha! She had explained how they met: "He picked me up in a bar in Pennsylvania where I worked and invited me to go to France." And her bored friends clutched their hands to their chests and swooned, and she said, "He didn't care that I was a twenty-year-old college dropout and I didn't care that he was forty and had five kids, a vasectomy, and three ex-wives!" Aww, they said. So romantic. (Was it?) "But," she went on, "that asshole never did take me to France." Then she felt bad for calling him an asshole.

A regatta of brightly colored sailboats glides past; para-sailers drift through the blue August sky. She tries to imagine her husband as a young boy playing on this beach, but she can't manage it. A gorgeous, sunburned Australian couple splashing nearby continue a conversation they began onshore—about whether or not a blind person could travel abroad alone. The conversation has now taken on the sharp, testy tones of an argument. Mary lifts an ear from the water to listen.

"So you've just arrived at the bus station in Nice," the man is saying. "And then what? We almost got hit by cars and *we* can see!"

"But that doesn't mean it's not possible. That doesn't mean that just because you're blind you should stay home."

"Yeah, it does," the man persists. "You *can* do whatever you want. People do stupid things all the time. But I'm saying that if you're blind, and you're traveling alone in a foreign country, one, you're an idiot, and B, you're going to get killed. Or at least mugged."

"So if *you* ever go blind, you're just going to stay home and do nothing?"

"No! But I'm not going to travel to a foreign country alone. Because that's common fucking sense."

The girl splashes away from him, as if she wants to swim all the way out to the cruise ship in the distance.

The man shouts: "Now deaf, sure. I mean, there's already a language barrier."

The woman turns, swims back. "Was it too much to hope that being here would turn you into a slightly different person?"

Apparently, it was. But it shouldn't be, Mary wants to say. In her eight days alone in France, she's become chatty with strangers, because that's what loneliness does to her. She's met old people and young people, Americans and Swedes and Canadians in Aix and Arles and Avignon. Loneliness and wine, that's what loosens her up.

"In my experience," she calls, breast-stroking toward the couple, "travel turns you more into the person you already are." She smiles. The woman looks horrified at having been not only overheard but also understood. The man says, "Well, maybe you're right."

"Honeymoon?" Mary presses.

"We are, yeah," says the woman. Her dark hair is so sleek that Mary wants to reach out and pet it. The top of her nose is sunburned.

"Me, too," Mary says cheerfully, before she can stop herself. "The honeymoon I never had, so twenty years later I'm here alone." The young man and woman are frowning; they want to swim away from her, this crazy lonely lady, so she says, "I'm a widow," and yes: they're still wary, they still want to get away from her, but now she makes some kind of sense.

"I'm so sorry," says the woman. She seems to have alighted on a rise of beach, standing instead of floating.

"But you're here," says the man.

"Better late than never," says Mary.

•

Ellen and Carrie parted ways after customs in Atlanta: Carrie headed for her flight home to Chicago, Ellen to Mississippi. They hugged briefly, then Carrie was disappearing down the escalator to the plane train, staring at her phone. Something occurred to Ellen: "Carrie!" she yelled. Carrie glanced up. "Did you ever pay that taxi driver?" But Carrie just frowned and then was gone.

Ellen's mother met her at the airport, which was more than she could say about her suitcase. "We'll call you when we find it," said the cheerful idiot behind the Delta counter. "Will you?" Ellen asked, and he said, "We'll sure try."

"What did you get me?" her mother demanded, as she drove past the flat Mississippi fields. The air conditioner huffed to little effect as the August glare baked the inside of the car.

"So much stuff," Ellen lied.

"And did you have a good time?" her mother asked, meaning: Did your successful older sister with the real job keep you from drinking too much and making a fool of yourself? "Did you see Carrie's presentation?" Carrie was a featured speaker at an International Conference on Something to Do with the Internet. Ellen had invited herself along, paying for her own ticket with the money she should have used for fall semester. While Carrie gave her presentation, Ellen was getting stoned with a guy named Ken, who'd given his presentation already and was "now just ready to chill-ax."

"I sure did," Ellen lied again. Oh, lying was so much easier than any kind of truth. "We had a great time, bonding and braiding each other's hair."

Her mother snorted.

Four days in a foreign country must have changed her, right? But it seemed as if there should be more evidence to reveal what this change might be: aside from a video of a woman's death, which Ellen would most definitely delete, but deleting it would mean looking at it. Wouldn't it? Or at least thinking about it. Jesus. Christ. Her stomach felt like a rotten apple. Worms and mush and a hard, bitter core. "I'm really jet lagged," she said. "I don't want to talk."

"Cranky much?" Her mother missed the exit toward town. "I think I should have turned back there," she said.

"It was fine. Whatever!" Ellen had moved in with her mother six months earlier, after dropping out of college, after her arrest for shoplifting. She'd almost convinced herself that waitressing was a viable career path.

But now she found herself thinking of Ryan, the guitar player in the band she sometimes sang (badly) in. He liked her. He had his own apartment. She began to feel her spirits lift a little. "It's nice to be home," she said, meaning: *It's nice to be back in the land of my familiar mistakes and I look forward to making many new, perhaps stupider ones.*

"Home again, home again, jiggety jig," her mother said.

•

The couple's names are Will and Breanna, and they met when they were children in Brisbane but only recently reconnected at a friend's house and fell in love and *voilà,* six months later here they are. "It seems fast," says Will, treading water. "But we've really known each other forever."

"I married Henri six weeks after we met," Mary says, adding a week.

"And *voilà*," says Breanna.

"He's a French professor," Mary continues. "I mean, he was. That's what he was. He spent his childhood in Nice. We never got a chance to go."

"Oh!" Breanna gives an annoying little shriek. "That's so romantic I can't stand it."

Will reaches over and dunks Breanna's head under water and she sputters angrily to the surface.

You two will divorce, Mary thinks. *And* voilà.

The sea is filling up with floating families shouting in French and Spanish and Russian. Crispy men clutching their bellies like great hairy crockpots. She'd been surprised by all the Russians and the menus in Cyrillic. But what better place to escape the Moscow snow? Earlier today, she wandered the grounds of the Cathedral of St. Nicholas, built in honor of a young tsarevich who expired at twenty-one from meningitis, the sea air having failed to cure him. Sea air, it turned out, could only do so much.

"My husband was much older than me." She's surprised at how easy it is to speak of Henri in the past tense; she feels her eyes spring with tears. The salt of the sea seems to be everywhere. Her shoulders are burning, but the water feels so kind. "Twenty years. He died of cancer," she adds, because she assumes they want to know but won't let themselves ask. "Pancreatic." She knows she's a terrible person, killing off her perfectly nice husband (well, not perfectly) but there's no way out of this now. Now she will always be the nice lady they met floating in the sea, a brave widow, a cautionary tale perhaps. "You remind me of one of those creatures that lure sailors to their deaths," she tells Breanna. "Not mermaids, the other things. What are those called?"

"Bitches," says Will.

Mary ignores him. "When you two get a divorce," she says to Breanna, "you should come here alone and meet someone kind."

Which is of course the wrong thing to say, and there's only so much you can forgive a lonely widow, she realizes, watching them swim away from her.

•

Ellen found herself thinking of the woman who'd died, making her up in her head: a thirty-two-year-old French-woman who had grown up in Nice and was heading to meet her new lover for drinks at the Negresco, crossing the street in the crosswalk like she was supposed to, obeying all the rules, and then: blammo. Gone.

Or she was a forty-year-old Italian woman, also meeting her lover for drinks at the Negresco (Ellen realized her imagination only went so far) but she was married and so was he, and it would all be a disaster anyway, but no more of a disaster than her current marriage. She'd married Carlo after only knowing him for six months, and her sister and mother both hated him, and her father would be rolling in his grave if she believed in any kind of afterlife.

Or she was a twenty-two-year-old woman from some-where in America, let's say California, a place Ellen wouldn't mind going. Maybe she and Ellen had similar lives, meaning that this woman's father also died when she was eight and her therapist seemed to think that was the cause of many of her problems, including her arrest for stealing all those bathing suits from Belk. She'd come to France to get away from her own stupid life and stupid problems, and then a taxi carrying Ellen and Carrie ran her over while she was crossing the street and she had no more problems again, ever. Her mother and her sister came from California—or no, they had the body shipped home. Her mother said, *She had so much potential*, and her sister said, *She was so much smarter than me.*

Ellen told herself she should watch the video for clues, but clues for what? She told herself she should delete it. But maybe it was better to carry it, like a talisman, a weight, a reminder of how much worse things could be. Soon she would watch it. It would be terrifying; it might even be art. Certainly it would be more meaningful than anything else she'd accomplished in her life, including her terrible sing-ing in that terrible band.

Within two weeks of returning from France, Ellen moved in with Ryan, the lead guitarist of the terrible band. He lived in a studio apartment above a hair salon on Main Street, and the smell of hair products wafted up through the vents. She wanted to be in love with him, but she couldn't quite convince herself. On a rainy October night, after their band played a nearly-empty bar in a nearly-empty town in the next county, she picked a fight that left them both with slapped-red faces. By the time her lost suitcase miraculously arrived in November, she'd already moved back in with her mother.

•

The newlyweds have disappeared into the crowd on the rocky beach. More couples splash past; the cruise ship in the distance toots its horn; an airplane circles, disappears toward the airport. There seems to be no lifeguard. Mary knows she should get out of this lovely water, write some postcards to mail before she flies home tomorrow. She bought ten of them—does she even know ten people? Her eyes sting from the salt. The Mediterranean is warmer than she'd expected, and much more crowded. So many families and couples and old people, everyone bobbing in the sea like survivors of a shipwreck—waiting for rescue but not really expecting it.

Or no: no reason to be morbid. Purgatory, then. Everyone just bobbing between one place and another.

She feels that in the past eight days, she has traveled not just through space but through seasons and centuries: an 1880s winter in Arles, a seventeenth-century spring in Avignon, and finally a futuristic summer in Nice. It's just weather, Henri would say, but she knows it's more than that. Each town has a soul, she might tell him. And now each of those souls is part of her own.

Yesterday, she walked through the alleys of Old Nice, through the smells of curry and sausage, the souvenir and flower shops. She was following, at a discrete distance, an elderly British couple who seemed to have left their spouses behind in Blackpool to have an affair. She was not entirely sure of this scenario, but it seemed plausible, and it suddenly seemed important to find out for certain. Was this something one did when one was eighty years old? Why not get a divorce? The children, if there were any, must be at least in their fifties. She heard the man say, "What did you tell your Jack?" and the woman replied, "Visiting Phyllis," which was apparently a hilarious idea, because he laughed and said, "Oh, Lord!" The woman asked, "You?" and he replied: "Visiting your mother," which made her howl. "No, some drivel about Reggie."

"Oh, Reggie," the woman sighed. And then they paused in front of a window featuring a pig torso stuffed with head cheese.

Mary lingered. She could say, "Do I know you?" She could say, "I'm a friend of Reggie's!" But she lost her nerve. The woman looked over at her and when Mary smiled, the woman pulled on the man's hand and they disappeared into the crowd.

Good for you, Mary thinks now. And best of luck to Reggie, Phyllis and Jack.

Her shoulders really are burning. She will get out of the water—clamor over those slippery, slippery stones—find her sandals and sundress on the pebbly shore and walk the three blocks to her hotel, and on the way she might find someone else to talk to, or she might not. She might stop for a glass of white wine and write a post card to Henri: *Having a lovely time.* Or: *Travel has changed me, and I don't know how.* Or: *Wish you were here. Hope to see you somewhere in the great big world again, someday.*

•

The suitcase looked like an artifact from some other life. It had arrived while Ellen was still sleeping, hungover from drinking too much tequila with Oliver, her manager, after her shift last night. They'd made out in the supply closet while the last few customers finished their steaks. She'd driven home drunk, stumbled into the house and puked in the hall toilet as quietly as she could. The doorbell had arrived like an alarm, an alert, a mantra drilling through her skull: wake up, get up, grow up. By the time she pulled open the front door, a car was driving away, and the suitcase was sitting there in the cold rain like an orphan.

"Mom?" Ellen called.

But maybe she didn't want her mother here to witness this. She felt as if she were excavating a cursed tomb as the memories of those four days in France came rushing back: too much wine on the plane to Paris, Carrie snapping at her as Ellen made her hungover way too slowly through Charles de Gaulle. They spent the first day in

Nice walking the hot streets, attempting and then aban-
doning small talk. Ellen bought a sketch pad and a book
about Matisse, written in French, which made Carrie roll
her eyes. They were sharing a room at the Westminster,
which was full of loud British tourists. They drank wine
and ate mussels and Ellen asked Carrie if she ever saw
Martin, her ex-husband, and Carrie said, "At least I didn't
get arrested for shoplifting damn bikinis," and things
went downhill from there.

Ellen had stalked alone through the streets and gotten lost and confused and someone tried to snatch her
purse. So much for the glamorous French Riviera! It was
hot and crowded and people were stupid there like they
were everywhere. And then she was chatting up some guy
named Ken and going off to his room to get stoned. He'd
wanted to do more, of course, but she lied and said, "I have
a boyfriend," and he said, "Whatever."

Where was beauty, where was art? Romance would
be nice, too, but it wasn't necessary. Just beauty and art
and . . . "Hope," she'd mumbled stonedly at Ken, handing
him the joint. And he said, "What?" and she said, "Never
mind. I just feel so fucking old, you know?" He shrugged,
because he was thirty, so he really did know about being
old. She felt tragic but not beautiful, and what was the
point of being tragic if you weren't beautiful?

Shampoo had opened and leaked on everything: all
the dresses and shoes and scarves from Monoprix, purchased with her mother's credit card. A new wave of
shame washed over her. The Matisse book was relatively
unharmed. She would give that to her mother to put on the
coffee table and never look at.

"Mom?" she called again. Her mother's car was in the
driveway. She was an ER nurse at the county hospital, and
now that Ellen thought of it, she should be at work by now.
Shouldn't she? It seemed as if she saw her mother only in
passing; they were poltergeist-roommates, drifting through
rooms and leaving cabinets open and lights on.

The back door was unlocked, the aluminum ladder against the side of the house—oh, her mother refused to hire anyone to clean out the gutters!—and her mother lay like a limp doll in the damp grass. Her eyes were closed. Her hands curled at her side. That's what happened: a woman was here one moment, gone the next. Ellen had been drifting, drifting, drifting and now she'd crashed ashore into adulthood—*Grow the fuck up,* Carrie had said, finding Ellen stoned in the bathtub—yes, crashed right onto the jagged, horrible shore of it. She could see it all with utter clarity, the way she hadn't at eight when her father had a heart attack. She would call 911, then call Carrie. There would be a coroner, a funeral director, a notice in the paper, flowers, fresh dirt in the neat cemetery lawn. Ellen's knees were damp, her face was wet, she knew this was somehow all her fault, and if she could rewind days, months, years, that's what she would do.

Her mother opened her eyes. "Oof," she said, pulling herself to a sitting position. "I think I took a little spill."

●

A man who looks vaguely like Henri splashes past, his silver-bald head flashing in the sun. Mary wonders if he has a younger wife at home—or maybe that very, *very* young woman in the blue bikini, roasting herself on a towel, is his wife. At least Mary has never worried about Henri having an affair. He told her he was through with crazy women. "Until you met me," she said, and he laughed.

Her life consists of faculty parties, a secretarial job, companionship and loneliness. Light and shadow. Is there any other way to live with someone else? She doubts it. Henri has taken her to his conferences in London, to Montreal, to Lisbon. But never here, the place where he was raised by parents who died when he was fifteen—first the father in a car accident, then his mother of heart failure. It suddenly strikes her how cruel she must seem, to want him to return to this place.

The silver-bald man has been joined by a solid-bodied, age-appropriate woman in a red one-piece. They seem to be speaking German, and Mary has a sudden flash of the two of them toiling up the Alps with walking sticks, gazing serenely over a *Sound of Music* landscape. She lifts a hand in greeting, calls, "Hello!" She wants to ask: Is there a certain depth of loneliness that's only possible with another person? Do you both feel it, like a weight pressing on you in the middle of the night? Do you ever wake up and look at each other and think: Where have you gone? "Hello!" she calls again, and they swim away.

She knows it's time to get out of the water and so, moments before her death, Mary climbs from the sea. She winces her way over the sharp and slippery stones, finds her yellow sundress and her sandals on the shore. Her room key still in her pocket. Her sunglasses tucked in one shoe. A hairy, deeply-red man in a white Speedo nods at her as he strides past. Two children fight over a yellow beach ball. She pulls her dress on over her damp bathing suit. Nothing terrible has happened yet, she tells herself; she is not a widow floating in the sea. Henri is at home. When she called him two days ago, he said, "I miss you," and she said, "You should." She was mean. She'd felt annoyed. Now she allows herself to consider the possibility that he missed her enough to buy a plane ticket and come here to surprise her. It could happen.

The wide boulevard opens up in front of her; behind her, the sound of the sea. She walks up the beach toward the Promenade des Anglais—Walk of the English? Something like that. She crosses halfway, to the grassy median; in the late afternoon light she can almost believe Henri really is waving from the other side of the street. He isn't, of course, but a trick of the light, she will tell him, is still a pretty good trick.

•

The nurses made a fuss over Ellen's mother, teasing: "Oh, Ruth, you clumsy-ass you!" Ellen's mother lay grinning, propped in a hospital bed, bandages on her twisted ankle and sprained wrist. Nothing was broken. Ellen thought of calling Carrie, then decided against it. She took her mother home, tucked her into bed and gave her the Matisse book and one of the Monoprix scarves she'd bought for herself. "That's so nice of you to think of me," her mother said, beaming.

Ellen poured herself a beer, rummaged through the cabinets for something to make for lunch. Tomato soup. Grilled cheese. The food of childhood. She called Oliver and told him she wouldn't be coming in for her shift later. "My mother was nearly *killed*," she said and felt her voice catch. She wanted to quit, but she thought of her mother's credit card bill, full of charges her mother didn't even ask about. "I want overtime this weekend," she said. She hung up before he could answer.

She finished her beer and took a breath. Her phone. The video. A woman's death. Here today, gone tomorrow. She needed to finally delete it, yes, but first she would watch it, blood and chaos and sirens—or no. What was playing before her eyes was none of those things. There was blue sky, and there were cars, a swirl of beach, and Carrie yelling for her to hurry, but she had left the camera on selfie mode so that all she'd captured was her own confused face, yelling, "But we're witnesses!"

There weren't even any sirens, not yet.

Seven Ravens

A week after their first and only date, Alexis called Ned and said, "I'm in the hospital."

"Are you okay?" said Ned, who was holding the phone to his ear while he pushed a shopping cart through Walmart. It was nine-thirty on a Saturday morning, and he'd made the mistake of forgetting that it was a home game day. The aisles were clogged with families in maroon T-shirts pushing carts stacked with Budweiser and chips.

"I'm *fine*," she said, as if being fine were something she could barely stand. She'd used the same tone when, at the end of their date, she'd said, "I suppose I'll call you." She hadn't, and—after the pang of being rejected by someone he hadn't really cared for had passed—that was fine with Ned. He'd only answered the phone because he hadn't recognized her number. "I need a favor, though."

And so Ned paused in the frozen meats aisle while Alexis explained to him that she'd been chopping onions, and chop chop chop, off went her finger, and if only she'd saved it they might be able to reattach it. "My left pointy finger," she said. "I'm right-handed but I'd still like to keep it, if at all possible." What she was asking, Ned realized as a tide of families flowed around him, was for him to go to her house—unlocked—and hunt around on the kitchen floor for her severed finger, and deliver it to the hospital. "On ice," she said, as if she were describing a seafood platter or a mixed drink.

He pushed his nearly-full cart into a crevasse between the car magazines and inspirational novels and left it there. He walked, swinging his keys, out into the bright September day, telling himself he was answering a noble call.

•

Alexis lived in a blue cottage in a student neighborhood five blocks from the university and a mile from Ned's own house. The porches of the homes around hers were littered with beer bottles and weather-beaten sofas; a plaster bulldog, the school mascot, crouched on her front step. He would not have expected her to be a school mascot kind of person. All he really knew about her was that she'd moved from Buffalo to Mississippi two months ago and was a new assistant professor in the psychology department. They'd been set up by Ned's colleague, Paul, a fellow web designer who had met her at a happy hour and insisted that she and Ned would hit it off. Which they did not.

Inside the house, he was struck by the piles of satin throw pillows and the smell of onions and melted wax. A splinter of light cracked through dark living room curtains. It was what you might expect from the home of a Wiccan priestess, and this impression was further conveyed by the bloody scene that greeted him in the kitchen. He felt as if he'd stumbled upon the aftermath of a very small murder: tiny pools of blood on the counter, a swath of splatter across the freezer, the glinting butcher knife on the Formica floor. No finger, thank God. But where could it be?

Ned had always been dizzy around blood, and now was no exception. He closed his eyes, then opened them. The left pointy finger, she'd called it, which he assumed was the index finger. But now he imagined it pointing at him from its hiding place, the companion to the finger she'd directed at him as she said, "I thought you'd be balder."

He tried to recreate the scene: chop chop chop, she'd said, and the finger had . . . had she actually said it had "flown right off"?

Apparently, it was gone. Maybe she'd tucked it into her purse? It occurred to him that her car was also gone, that she'd driven herself two miles to the hospital. It seemed like a brave feat, and his heart warmed to her the way it hadn't on their date during the awkward spaghetti dinner at a strip mall restaurant.

He peeked into the sink, under the kitchen table. The blood splatter on the freezer door might be a clue, and sure enough, when he rocked the refrigerator away from the wall, there it was, bigger and pinker than he'd expected, resting in a pile of gray dust. From the size of it, she was left with about a half inch of finger stump. The thought of retrieving it (with a broom? Salad tongs?) made him go fuzzy around the sides of his vision. No, he thought. No.

He arrived at the hospital to find her sitting on the side of a tidy white bed, groggy from painkillers and holding a swathed hand up in the air as if she had a question to ask in class. "Well?" she asked.

"No luck," he said.

•

It was something that, if their relationship persisted, would probably haunt him, which is why he was reluctant to accept her offer of a dinner to repay him for looking for her finger. "God knows," she said, "it could have gone down the sink! I was pretty frantic, and there was so much blood."

Their second date, as he had reluctantly come to accept it was, took place at a college hangout on Main Street, a hamburger and beer joint that was already full of douchebags at seven-thirty on a Friday night. Ned hadn't gone out on a Friday night in more than a year, since his breakup

with Brenda. Brenda was a graphic designer in his department, Agricultural Communications. They'd bonded over
jokes about teaching farm animals to text message, and
he'd been charmed by her snorty laugh. She had a three-
year-old son whom she was still nursing—"Don't judge
me!" she'd warned him, which made him judge her. She
went back to her ex-husband in Tuscaloosa, which was a
relief to them both.

Ned and Alexis were sitting outside on the balcony, and
she kept waving at people walking by on the street below.
"Hi, Karen, hi Richard!" How did she know so many
people?

"Oh, I'm just on so many committees," she said. "You
know, the life of an academic!"

Ned was not an academic, so he didn't know, but he
said, "Sure." He supposed he should ask about the finger,
still swathed in gauze, but so far he'd done a good job of
ignoring it—as if it were a pimple or a hairy mole. Look
away, look away. "So," he said, and then couldn't think of
anything else.

On their first date, they'd covered the basics: they were
both in their early forties, childless and never married. She
was from New York, he was from Maryland. She was not
unattractive, which is how Ned supposed he could also
be described. Thick curly hair, eyes brown and blank as a
doll's. Stunningly straight teeth. Her breasts seemed ample.

He sat back and chewed on his hamburger and listened
as she explained, in tedious detail, about her lab and her
students and how she had to keep changing her syllabus
because "new ideas keep coming to me, you know?"

He nodded. She hadn't asked him about his own job.
Nobody really cared about the Agricultural Communications website except for him and Paul.

"You know what?" she said, wiping her mouth with a
greasy napkin. "You're going to marry me."

"Excuse me?" said Ned.

"You heard me," she said.

•

"I saw you two the other night," Paul said at work on Monday. "Dining al fresco at Mugshots. So it's going well?" He waggled his eyebrows. Paul and his wife Rachel had three kids and were always inviting Ned to come to church picnics, which he never did. It struck him for the first time that maybe Paul was so interested in other people's love lives because he no longer had one of his own.

"She's kind of moody and steamroller-like," Ned said. "I don't do much of the talking, and she has no interest in my life."

"But she's nice," said Paul. "Right?"

Ned wondered what in his description of her had gone through Paul's brain computer and spit out the word NICE. "I suppose," he said, then ran off to see the IT people about a broken database. It seemed as if his world was full of broken databases, none of which he had control over, all of which he needed in order to function in his capacity as employee or human being.

For instance, a normal human being, after being threatened with marriage on the second date by someone he did not like, would reasonably decline a third date. Reasonably, a person with an intact database would not say, "How about going to the football game with me next weekend?" Especially when he had never in his life been to a college football game. And yet this is what had happened as they stood on the sidewalk of Main Street. Alexis had pouted down at her car keys, then kissed him on the cheek. "You got it," she said.

•

The following weekend, Alexis led him through the maze of maroon and white tents on the drill field to the psychology department's tailgate party, a series of blue tables set up under a maroon tent, where a mustached man was doling out heaps of pulled pork on Coronet paper plates. "This is my boyfriend," Alexis announced. "Ned. He does web design."

"Ned of the Web," said a red-haired woman with cat eye glasses.

And so he was Alexis' boyfriend, Ned of the Web, as she took him around to meet graduate students and her colleagues and "my experiments," she said, nodding toward an Asian man and a Black woman, both chewing heartily on pulled pork. "See, I give my subjects a paragraph containing controversial information—like, about global warming—and then show them Gary's face as the one who said it, then show them Julia's face, and then show them"— she pointed toward a blonde, tan Ken doll standing by the beer cooler—"Derek's face, and they determine how reliable the information is." She forked a heap of potato salad into her mouth but kept talking.

"I'm sorry, what?" said Ned.

"I said, Derek wins every time. Most reliable."

"Well," said Ned, "global warming isn't exactly controversial."

She shrugged. Her eyes were so dark you almost couldn't find the pupil; he was reminded of a hamster he'd had in middle school. A flutter of orange leaves blew past; it was a warm September day, the sky turning the thick gold of late afternoon. Ned accepted beers and let himself be led around and introduced. Apparently, the finger was part of the story now—"He couldn't find it!"—and she demonstrated, holding up her hand with the now-bandageless stump.

"How about a knuckle sandwich?" yelled somebody.

Ned had another beer.

The lawn was full of shadows; tailgaters were streaming toward the stadium. He became aware of Alexis beside him. He was not cut out for this, he wanted to tell her. He was not Ned of the Web. But instead he said, "How is it?"

She understood immediately. "Throbs sometimes. Typing is harder. So is driving. It kind of sucks." There was silence. Then: "She said off-handedly. Get it? I thought of that yesterday."

"Good one," said Ned. He was aware of her slightly musky scent. He was drunk; he was tired and lonely. "Do you want to go to the coast with me next weekend?"

•

With Brenda, he'd done some wooing—flowers, gentle back rubs. Toys for the kid. Tenderness. That was what was missing with Alexis, but it didn't seem to be expected. Sex, apparently, was expected—and he wasn't opposed to it, as he discovered the following weekend. She was pliant and murmuring, reaching toward him on her Bugs Bunny sheets. Later, he'd gone to the kitchen for a drink of water, and the humming of the refrigerator had startled him— but surely it couldn't still be *under* there, could it? Surely a mouse or something—

After that, she spent the night at his house (he told her he was allergic to her fabric softener). They never did end up going to the coast. She always had something going on at her lab that she couldn't get away from. On the phone she was terse and distracted, sometimes hanging up midsentence. Days would pass and he would almost forget about her, and then she would call to inform him that she was coming over, or that he was taking her to dinner, or— in early October—that she was coming over to cook dinner for him. She didn't ask what he might like, or if he might be allergic to anything.

He could barely watch as she sliced the tomatoes with terrifying alacrity. "I know, I know," she sang, as the silver knife flashed. "Stop cringing; I'm being careful." It occurred to him that he had been cringing for weeks now and couldn't seem to stop.

•

Alone, Ned used to wake up each morning feeling squashed into the mattress. *I am full of sorrow,* he would murmur to himself. But now he'd stopped murmuring about sorrow. Once, driving to work, he realized he was saying, "Bap bap bap," over and over: nonsense. But pleasant nonsense. Maybe that was enough?

Sometimes he let his mind drift forward to the moment when he would take Alexis' mangled hand in his and slide a ring on her finger, doing his best to avoid looking at the stump. He thought of his favorite childhood prank: the gift box with the hole in it, the ketchup-ed finger lying on cotton, rising up like a cobra. His mother's scream.

"Things are serious," Paul said, finding Ned in his office staring miserably at his tented fingers.

"When aren't things?" said Ned. "Nothing connects." The website was a huge mess. The links were all broken; the photo of a pig led to an article about bull insemination. Linda, the graphic designer who had replaced Brenda, kept taking time off for her sick child, and the work she did turn in was all garish primary colors and Helvetica font. The database manager wouldn't return Ned's emails. Why wasn't anyone at least trying?

"I mean with Alexis. You seem happy." Paul rapped his knuckles on Ned's desk as if to ward off bad luck.

Ned said, "I'm confused. That sometimes works the same way."

Alexis had never again mentioned getting married, and he was beginning to understand that it had been some kind of joke—or perhaps an experiment. More and more, he got the feeling that some graduate student was about to leap out from behind a shrub with a clipboard and ask him to sign a human subject consent form.

•

Her parents were coming down from Albany for a visit. "They've never been to the South," said Alexis. "They're excited to drink sweet tea and eat catfish. Can you convince your parents to come next weekend, too? Wouldn't that be great?"

"My parents hate sweet tea and catfish," Ned said. Ned's parents lived in south Florida, divorced and remarried and, as his father once said, "Just splashing around in our pre-death years." When Ned visited, he spent half the time in Boca with his father and Minnie, playing miniature golf and drinking martinis; and half in Miami with his mother and Jude, volunteering at soup kitchens and repairing other people's houses. His brother lived in Orlando, but he had stopped visiting their parents because "it makes my brain explode." There was no longer any membrane connecting his parents' worlds unless that membrane was Ned. He'd not mentioned Alexis' existence to either of them.

Alexis' parents had been high school sweethearts, married for fifty years. Her mother was a smaller, plumper version of Alexis and her father was gaunt and grinning, his gray hair sticking out like the plumage of an ancient goose. They had heard all about Ned of the Web, had seen his website ("All I ever wanted to know about cow dung but was afraid to ask," said her father), and of course knew about the finger. They sat at a big round table at a restaurant popular with the graduation and prom crowd, and over her plate of half-eaten catfish, Alexis' mother peered at the stump through her reading glasses, teeth clenched.

"I can't imagine how you did that," she said at last.

"She always was a klutz," said her father. "That time on the bicycle."

"Woodshop," her mother said.

"Balance beam," said her father.

"Her prom date slammed her hand in the car door— other hand, right? He left her crying by the curb."

"He would have married you, Alexis, but you're such a difficult person," said her father.

"Ever since you were a baby," said her mother.

Alexis was staring straight ahead; she had been chewing the same bite of salad for a very long time.

"I fell off my bike, too," Ned offered.

Her father grinned.

Later, when Ned and Alexis were in his bed, she rolled toward him and said, "My parents should have gotten divorced about twenty years ago. They had the potential to be good people."

He thought that was the most frightening thing he'd ever heard, but he said nothing, just pulled her closer. Sometimes he thought that he might actually love her, and then he thought it was all a mistake. He had already grievously betrayed her. He had nothing to offer. He had one friend, if he counted Paul, and a small house, a fifteen-year-old car and a job that had bored him for six years. His life, he thought, was like global warming: everything melting, everything floating away. The polar bears crying on their ice floes. Some people (like Paul) might argue that it was a natural process, but Ned knew it was man-made, by him.

•

The ring had appeared in his sock drawer as if through some divine mystery. He could almost forget that he'd gone to Jane's Jewelry on Main Street and bought it—a tiny ruby, four hundred dollars—standing there with a frowning boy who couldn't be older than twenty. "Mine likes emeralds," said the boy. "What does yours like?"

"Mine doesn't care," said Ned, thinking: *Ha, I win.*

He felt that disembodied finger poking at him, poking and poking. Though sometimes, more and more, he thought he might have started to forget, as if he'd absorbed that missing appendage, that space, into his own body, where it floated around inside his ribcage, in the general proximity of his heart.

•

In early November, he drove to Alexis' house down the damp, leaf-smashed streets to pick her up for a Thursday night drinks date. She had been more stressed than usual; her research assistant had bungled some data. A publication was in jeopardy. At night, she muttered in her sleep and he went out to his sofa to watch crime dramas on Netflix, then to his job to make the cow info, pig info, and horse info appear in their correct places. But there had been a breakthrough: Linda's kid was no longer sick so her designs had improved; IT had finally given Ned the logins he needed to make changes on his own, and his boss had actually given him a thumbs-up as they passed in the corridor yesterday.

The sky was turning the dusky gray of early evening; ravens wheeled in the trees above him—or no, they were American crows. He'd learned that linking the Mississippi Birds website to the Wildlife and Fisheries site. They perched on the bare trees above Alexis' house, seven of them, calling to each other as Ned slammed out of his car and made his way to her porch, past the bulldog statue that had surprised him on his first visit. She'd told him later that she didn't care about bulldogs, she just wanted to look like she did.

The front door was open, and through the screen he could hear music—something both jangling and aching. "Hello, lover!" Alexis cried. Her cheeks were flushed; she was wearing a red, celebratory-looking dress he had never seen before.

"Good news about the publication?" he said.

She turned in a circle, then padded over in her bare feet and kissed him. For some reason, there was a mayonnaise jar on the kitchen counter that seemed to contain a large caterpillar, something destined for life as a gray and frantic moth. "Doesn't the house smell *clean?*" she said. She waited. Her eyes were too bright.

"Yes," he said.

"I was cleaning." She stood before him, arms clasped around herself. "And there it was—behind the fridge. Who would have thought it was there the whole time? We should bury it. In your yard, I think. And plant a sunflower over it. Yes?"

The house smelled of lemons, like a forest of fruit trees. He thought of fairy tales, of Hansel locked in his cage. He thought of his magic trick finger in its tiny coffin. Alexis was beaming. Next to the horrible jar there was a packet of sunflower seeds. There would be no flowers in his yard, he understood, and by the time they bloomed in hers—next to the bulldog statue—he would not be here to see them. "Coward," she would call him later on the phone, and he would nod and say nothing while she chanted, "Coward, coward, coward," like the call of a bird.

"My darling," he said now. He stepped toward her, and for the first and last time he took her left hand and brought it to his lips. He kept his eyes open as he kissed the pale, scarred flesh. And then he turned away from the jar, away from Alexis; the doors of her house seemed to swing open for him, and he was outside. The air was cool, the seven crows watched him. In the musty sky, thin, glowing clouds were aligning themselves into signs: keys, fingers, everything pointing him away from here and from the strange and tender thought that the missing part of her was the only part he could have loved.

The Age of Discovery

We're on the third stop of our Lisbon food tour when I realize that someone is missing. There were eleven of us, and now there are ten. I say to my husband, "Where is that man?" and he says, "What man?" We're crammed into a little shop with dried and unidentifiable carcass parts hanging from the ceiling. A man in an apron is slicing off pieces of flesh for us to eat.

"That man who said he was from Germany. Sixty-ish, glasses."

"There wasn't anybody from Germany," my husband says.

The tour guide passes around slices of meat, and I count the number of slices: eleven. I count the number of people: ten.

"Oh right," my husband says. "That man. I don't know. Isn't he here?"

Then the tour guide takes the last piece of meat so there isn't an extra slice after all. My head aches. My feet ache. It's been raining since we arrived this morning, since we dragged our rolling bags over the cobblestones and up steep hills that didn't look like hills on the map. The map gave no indication of hills.

The tour guide has a small mustache; he's wearing a lanyard and a red rain slicker. He's very enthusiastic about the meat, which is salty and slippery. He kisses his fingers at it. Now there are tiny plastic cups of port wine going around. We're crammed elbow to elbow in the shop. So maybe the man from Germany is outside? Maybe he's claustrophobic? He seemed lonely, quiet. He was the only person on the tour by himself.

There are two gray-haired sisters from Dallas who seem friendly, unlike the young Italian couple who hang back and whisper to each other like mean seventh graders. "Do you remember that man?" I say to one of the sisters, trying not to jam her with my elbow. I drink the port too fast. It tastes like sweet prunes. "The man who was by himself?"

"From Australia," she says, nodding. "Where'd he go?"

"I thought he was from Sweden," says her sister. "Wowee. This port is going right to my head."

The tour guide is shoving through our group toward the doorway. "Come along, family!" He calls us his family because we're all in this together. Also, he said he couldn't possibly remember our names.

"I'm going to ask him about the missing man," I tell my husband, who looks annoyed. Maybe he's annoyed because he left his umbrella back in the hotel, even though I told him to take it. Or maybe he's annoyed because his phone keeps buzzing, and I keep telling him to ignore it.

Our group flows out into a wide street lined with department stores and restaurants, people drinking under dripping awnings, tourists with their rolling bags. The March rain has slowed to a drip; patches of Portuguese sky—which seems bluer than Mississippi sky—are glowing through the clouds. The tour guide says, "Watch out for pickpockets!" and we clutch at our purses and wallets. I know all about the pickpockets from reading Tripadvisor. I bought myself a purse that's designed to foil them with its zippered interior, and I bought my husband a shirt with a secret pocket for his wallet. I hear his phone buzz from the non-secret pocket in his jeans.

"*Don't*," I say, and then I head toward the tour guide who's leading us up a cobblestone hill, because Lisbon is mostly cobblestone hills, it turns out. Up and down, up and down. "Excuse me," I say. "Do you know what happened to that man who was by himself? I think he was from Germany? Because he's not here."

The guide stops, frowns, counts. "Family!" he shouts. "Are we missing one?" He counts again. "We have ten, and I'm eleven. Is anyone not here?" The Italian couple are far ahead, as if they don't care anymore. The Dallas sisters are staring at a menu on a window. There's a Swedish husband and wife and a British husband and wife, all white and white-haired and at least sixty years old. My husband and I are both fifty, and for the first time in years I feel youngish even though my knees ache, even though I wish the young Italian couple weren't snubbing us.

"I think we should go back and find him," I say, feeling gallant. "Retrace our steps."

The tour guide seems mad at me. "There are eleven people," he says, pointing to himself and then counting the rest of us again, pointing up the hill at the disappearing Italians. "Family! This way." And we trudge on.

I say to the Swedish couple, "Do you remember that man?" The Swedish couple speak perfect English, and earlier they were talking to the Italians in perfect Italian.

The Swedish wife points at the British man. "Him?" she says, and my husband says, "Right, he's here," and then his phone buzzes again and I say, "Don't!"

•

By the time we get to the fourth stop on the food tour, we're down to eight. The Italian couple wandered away, and we watched as they vanished around a bend and over a hill. The fourth stop is a wine bar with a big table set with bread and olive oil and Azorean cheese and red wine. The only other customers are a middle-aged couple wearing matching American flag sweaters like you can buy at Old Navy.

My husband shows me his phone. He has nineteen missed calls from No Caller ID and nineteen text messages, also from No Caller ID. The messages are all like this:

Don't be afraid!

A very important person is calling you!

I cannot hurt you through the digital airwaves.

I check my own phone: nothing. I don't get the No Caller ID calls. And of course, our daughter hasn't called, either. She's seventeen and staying with my mother so she won't run away again. "I don't need a babysitter, and I didn't run away," she protested, and I pointed out that when you're on national news for vanishing with your forty-five-year-old biology teacher for twelve days, then yes, that counts as running away. The biology teacher's name is Mr. Handley. How we'd joked about that name. We said, "Don't let Mr. Handley get handsy!" and Leslie rolled her eyes and made gagging noises. Mr. Handley had a ring of hair around his bald spot, like a monk. During parent-teacher conference night, he told us Leslie was a smart student who was making B's but could be making A's. We came home and told her this and she said, "Oh, I *know* how to make A's," and we laughed uncomfortably.

The British couple is sitting directly across from us, like we're on a double date. The wife says, "We've never left our cat alone for this long," and gives her husband a worried look. Her husband says, "Oh, nonsense, he'll be fine," and his wife says, "Peter's cat died of loneliness after three days." Her husband sighs heavily.

"Our daughter might die of boredom," I say, but they don't laugh. We dip bread into olive oil; the cheese is cold and sweet enough to make my teeth ache. The tour guide stands and tells us how to say *cheers* in Portuguese and we all try to say it; we clink our glasses. He tells us about the Age of Discovery, Vasco da Gama, Prince Henry the Navigator, Magellan, the spice trade, the slave trade. He tells us about the earthquake of 1755, how it destroyed most of the city, including the very place where we are now drinking wine and eating cheese. Everything gone, broken, turned to rubble in seconds. And as if that wasn't enough, there was a fire, and as if *that* wasn't enough, there was a tsunami. I feel as if I can relate.

"Do you like living here?" pipes one of the Dallas sisters from the end of the table.

"Oh, yes. I grew up here," the tour guide says. "I have a beautiful wife, four beautiful children. Of course, there's corruption in the government, but it's not polite to talk about politics! Right, family?" I feel like he's giving the Americans a disappointed look, but I could be imagining things. The man and woman in the Old Navy shirts are gathering their coats. At least we're not wearing American flag T-shirts, I think, but when they speak to each other, it's in some language that definitely isn't any variation of English. I can't even tell what it could be.

The tour guide seems to be weeping. My husband shoves me and raises an eyebrow, but I feel like weeping, too—all this wine, all this history of disaster and exploration and exploitation! "Maybe we shouldn't have come," I murmur, the first time I've said this out loud. But I don't say it loudly enough for him to hear me, so he doesn't.

•

Mr. Handley's wife was the one to call and tell us what was happening—or what had already been happening, without anybody knowing about it. My husband is a child psychologist and I'm an accountant, and yet we'd failed to put two and two together. (This clever observation came from a blonde woman on Fox News.) But what was the evidence, really? The music playing in her room, the giggling on the phone? The newly painted fingernails, the haircut, the whistling—since when did she whistle? *Leslie's got a crush,* I told my husband, and we knew better than to pry. We trusted her. We didn't snoop through her social media. Her grades were great—she was even getting A's in Mr. Handley's class! So when his wife called on a Friday afternoon to say, "Stuart's taken her somewhere," in a flat, low voice, I just thought: *Who the hell is Stuart?*

The sightings began immediately: at a Sprint Mart in Jackson, a campground in Alabama, an Applebee's in Chattanooga. My husband and I cried and blamed each other and then cried and blamed ourselves. Yes, we'd had a rough time recently. He had an affair with a colleague, I moved out for a few days, then back, but Leslie—she was fine. She didn't drink or do drugs or run with a fast crowd. Or any crowd. Wasn't that odd, now that we thought about it, that she didn't actually have *any* friends? No one invited her over after school; no one came around on the weekend.

And when we did snoop, finally, there it all was: the topless photos she'd sent to *Stuart,* the shirtless photos he'd texted back. *I want to lick your everything,* she'd texted, and he texted back a heart emoji. *I can't stand not being with you.*

When can we be together?
When?
When?
Soon.

•

The smell of marijuana drifts by as we troop across a city square. High above us, the statue of a man on horseback stares toward the sea. By the time we've crossed the square, we've been offered drugs three times and lost another couple: the Brits, waving us on as they turn back, probably to call home and check on their cat. A yellow electric tram rolls past crammed with faces, coats crushed against the windows. Our tour guide shouts: "This is tram number 28! It is very popular with pickpockets!"

We all reflexively clutch at our purses and wallets.

"I wanna go on that," says one of the Dallas sisters. She looks a little woozy, and I notice now that she's not even wearing real shoes: just sandals and damp woolen socks.

"Not me," I say. "No way."

"But it's what tourists do," my husband says. "And we're tourists."

"Tourists are idiots," I say as we follow the tour guide through a blue doorway into a café where a squat man behind the counter is pouring *vinho verde* into tiny goblets.

"So why'd y'all come to Lisbon?" the sock-wearing sister asks as we sip the wine. There is a complicated answer to this question: because my grandfather was Portuguese. But also: because I told my husband he owed me this, after his stupid affair. Because our daughter came back after disappearing for almost two weeks so we didn't cancel. "I'm not sure," I say at the same time that my husband says, "Why not?"

"Why not?" agrees one of the sisters, and the other sister chugs down her wine and says nothing.

The Swedish woman says, "This is much more food than I expected," as the squat man passes around a plate of fried codfish. "Oh, this is delicious. We love codfish in Sweden." Her husband just nods and smiles. There are two hunched old women eating soup at a small table in the back. A Black couple comes in with their rolling suitcases; they order *vinho verde,* drink it fast and roll away. The tour guide is telling us about the history of this café, how it's mentioned in a fado song. My head feels cotton-packed. My husband takes out his phone and shows it to me:

How are you?

I am thinking of you!

My husband is staring at the phone like he wants to punch it.

"It's not him," I say. "It's a robot, or whatever. A bot."

Mr. Handley—Stuart—never contacted us. So why would he do it now? He took Leslie to a campground in Tennessee and a concerned camper notified the police because Leslie "looked scared."

"I wasn't scared," she insisted later. "I was happy for once in my goddamn life." When I asked if he hurt her, she said, "Of course not." When I asked if he had sex with her, she said, "What do you think?" and burst into tears. Then: "No, no, he didn't. I wanted to, but he wouldn't. How do you think that makes me feel?" That seemed like a lie. Her therapist is a woman named Joan, a solid, smiling woman with bifocals and gray hair who wears paperclip necklaces fashioned by her grandchildren. Of course, Joan won't tell us anything. The medical doctor examined her and said there was no "trauma." I said, "Of course there's trauma!" and she smiled at me kindly.

Mr. Handley sprinted through the trees as the police closed in. He's been spotted in Nashville, Memphis, and Sydney. Not Lisbon. And yet, I think I see him everywhere. It's nonsense. When I first saw the gray-haired man from Germany, I thought: Could that be him, in disguise? Come all this way just to fuck with us? I knew better than to tell my husband this.

The tour guide is singing now in a deep, heartbroken voice. He stops and clears his throat. "A little fado," he says. "But very little. Here's a word. *Saudade.* It means a longing for something that does not exist. That's a good Portuguese word for you."

The Swedes have, miraculously, just realized they know two people standing at the bar: neighbors from their village! Isn't the world full of delightful surprises? Our Swedish couple and the other Swedish couple fall into conversation in Swedish, so it's just my husband and me and the Dallas sisters who follow the tour guide out into the damp evening air. A light rain spits. I hear my husband's phone buzz from his pocket.

"Turn it off," I say, but he ignores me. I'd told him to change his number. I had said, *Why would he contact you and not me?* And he said, *Because I'm the father. I'm the goddamn child psychologist father. I'm the one that fucked up.*

"This way, family," says the tour guide. He seems sad. We walk together, one drunken family, past shops and bars and squealing trams to another square where a crowd has lined up in front of a hole-in-the-wall bar. Three long-haired men are playing electric guitars to a group of tourists who sing along to "Mustang Sally." "I will return," the tour guide says, sounding like a brave explorer, and disappears into the crowd.

"I don't know if he'll come back," I say. "Do you think so?"

One of the Dallas sisters—the one wearing actual shoes—says, "I haven't been with a man in two years, since my divorce. I thought I'd be fine, but your body just starts craving another body." Her sister pats her on the arm. "I took judo lessons just to have a man throw himself on top of me," she continues. "But that was the only thing I enjoyed about it, and honestly, it made me feel too damn old."

"I didn't know you took judo," her sister says in consoling tones. Then: "That woman is about to get robbed."

We watch four pickpockets hover near a woman whose backpack flaps open. We watch as one of the men dips his hand in and out and then he flows back into the crowd without the woman noticing a thing. "I suppose we could have warned her," I say, and the sisters just shrug. My husband says nothing. "How would you feel?" I say to him. "If your *phone* got stolen?"

Our tour guide has returned bearing a bottle of a cherry liqueur called *ginjinha* and five tiny plastic cups. "Watch out for the pickpockets," he says as he pours us shots, but we are worldly now, we don't need to be warned. It's so easy to see them when you know how to look.

My husband takes out his phone and shows me what it says:

I am thinking of you!!
Do you miss me?
I wish to talk to you.
I wonder if you think of me.
"Jesus," I say. "That is one insecure bot."

The tour guide passes the bottle and we all drink shots and then more shots, like a hobo family. The liqueur is a sweet, burning cinnamon. I chew a sour cherry, and it makes the inside of my mouth vibrate. I toss the pits toward the pickpockets. *I see you,* I say to them with my eyes as I aim the pits. But they don't see me. They don't see my husband with his phone and his secret pocket. I watch and say nothing as they swarm toward a man carrying his wallet in his back pocket like an idiot; I watch as one of the pickpockets does exactly what pickpockets do, and the wallet-less man just laughs and takes a selfie.

The air has turned cool, and it makes me feel sober. But also, I feel like I could sing a fado song in Portuguese, as if there's something atavistic scrambling up and out of me. My grandfather never spoke Portuguese at home, so my mother never learned it, but I think I can almost understand it. I'm about to ask the tour guide to speak Portuguese to me when the sock-wearing sister says, "My feet are cold but the rest of me is hot." Her sister says, "I'm tired. Let's get out of here."

I watch as the sock-sister tips the tour guide ten euros. "Thanks for a lovely time," she says, and the two women walk off across the square, past the musicians and the back-packers.

"This is what happens with families," the tour guide says. He pours me the last of the liqueur; it's mostly cher-ries plopping into the little plastic cup. My husband has stepped away and is checking his goddamn phone. "I will miss you all," the tour guide says, and before I can tip him, he's vanished into the crowd. My husband is still glaring at his phone, so I take out my own and call my mother, who answers the way she always does: "What?"

"How's Leslie?" I ask, and I have to repeat it twice because the blues music is so loud and raucous, with cheers coming even from the pickpockets.

"She's fine. What time is it there?"

"I have no idea," I shout. "She's fine? She's there?"

"Of course she's here. We just ordered Domino's."

Sometimes I wonder if my mother even fully understands what happened. It occurs to me that none of us really explained it to her. She might think Leslie just stayed out too late with a boy. She never reads or watches the news because it makes her anxious.

"Tell her I say hi," I shout twice, and then give up and end the call.

My husband is standing beside me. "You drank it all," he says. I realize I'm still holding my little plastic cup. "Do you want to know what he's saying now?" he asks.

"No," I say, but he holds out the phone.

Always on my mind.

I will not hurt you!!!

But why will you not answer my calls, my dear friend?

"This is just fucking absurd," I say. I toss my little plastic cup on the ground and it skitters away, and I feel bad for littering in Lisbon. "You need to change your number! It's just generating random shit. It'll keep doing it forever because it's a robot."

"What if I answer?" he says. "The next time it rings?"

"Someone will ask if it's you, and you'll say yes, and then they'll have your voice recorded saying yes and you'll get charged for something. It's a scam. But sure, fine, answer it."

The sky looks bruised. It's a heartbroken sky, the moon is crying tears. I long for something that doesn't exist. But mostly, I want the phone to ring, so I can answer it and say, "Fuck off, motherfucker," and let them capture my voice saying that. Or maybe even singing it: the worst fado song ever. But it doesn't ring.

"Where's our hotel?" my husband asks, even though he knows where it is. We hiked down the steep hills of Alfama from our hotel with the blue curtains and the view of the castle. "We can take the pickpocket tram," he says. "It goes right past it."

"No," I say. "We can Uber." We're walking across another square—or is it the same one from earlier? A statue man on horseback far above us. The streets are clogged with tiny cars. Another Tram 28 clangs by, and squeals to a stop. I say, "I don't want to," but my husband is already standing in line to board and digging out euros from his jacket.

We shove toward the back, past entire families, like refugees seeking a better life. Well, I think, who isn't? My husband grabs a pole as the tram heaves into motion; we can't even see out the windows. My pickpocket-proof purse is digging into my stomach. I'm aware of all its zippers, closed. The air is tight and hot, and my face feels full of wool. The tram is climbing a hill, dinging, careening around a corner; we all sway against each other. I realize that I can pretty easily reach into my husband's not-secret pocket and pull out his phone, so I do, and he doesn't even notice, because he doesn't notice the things he should. I am a pick-pocket, I think with delight as my husband leans forward and says into my ear, "When do you think we get off?"

"I'm suffocating," I say.

His phone is in my hand, between my fingers, and I feel it drop, I'm stepping on it, and then it's sliding away, or trampled, it's gone, the tram stops and the doors open, and more people come and go, and I need air, I need something, and I say, "Come on," and push my way out the doors, into the lights and the cool night. The doors close and the tram clangs and moves on, taking my husband with it.

I watch the tram go down a hill and around a corner. I follow it, careful not to twist my ankle on the cobblestones; I watch it stop again and wait to see who gets off.

I will tell my husband: *You should have been more careful.*

I'll say: *Don't worry.*

It occurs to me that he might not even realize I'm gone, but no: there he is, at the bottom of the hill.

Or I'm pretty sure it's him.

The rain has started up again, so it's hard to tell for sure if the man walking up the hill toward me is someone I know, or just someone I think I know.

The Celebrity

The rumors were true: the Celebrity was in town—*our* town—to film her reality show, the one we hated but couldn't stop watching. She had actually been spotted, had been tweeted about, had posed for pictures in front of the Happy Cuts barber shop. Reports so far indicated that she was nice, even though on TV she was notoriously not nice. She'd had lunch at the BBQ Shack, *our* BBQ Shack, where we had after-church slaw and hushpuppies, where our children had birthday parties, where our sports fans watched the playoff games.

We drove around town in the heat, windows rolled down, looking for her, or for her cameras, or just a glimpse of that glossy raven hair. We drifted through red lights and stop signs; all over town there were near-collisions, laughed off with, "I was looking for *her!*"

There was a lottery to be part of her television show—to be a background diner, or a browsing customer, or a passer-by, and those of us lucky enough to be chosen signed ten-page contracts and confidentiality agreements: *We are allowed to use your image/silhouette/voice in perpetuity.* We mused on the possibility of that actually happening: our images, voices, silhouettes surviving long after our deaths, into perpetuity, that glimmering land inhabited by movie stars and singing sensations—and now, by us.

She was here because our town had made the bottom of various worst-in-the-country lists. Our garbage was especially putrid; our produce was extraordinarily limp. Our boutiques were musty with the fashions of yesteryear. Our children ran wild in the streets, smoking and stealing, and their parents went sporadically to dead-end jobs and spent the rest of the time drinking in dim bars.

On her TV show, the Celebrity breezed into sad towns and humiliated the townspeople, made old people cry, smacked some babies around, and mocked pets and automobiles, all while looking absolutely gorgeous in gold high heels and white dresses. She'd bring in construction crews to knock down buildings and rebuild them. She'd put shy children on parade floats and teach dogs to read simple history books. She'd turn coffee shops into wine bistros, add a seashore or a mountain, turn a mill town into a resort town, and combine single-parent families into blended Brady Bunch configurations—all in the course of four days. Before she left, she'd dole out some white dresses to the women, toss some red bow ties to the men, and new collars to the cats and dogs.

"Goodbye," she would call as she rode out of town on her motorcycle. "I'm on to the next dump."

•

We adjusted quickly to the cameras following us. It began to seem completely natural. Had it ever *not* seemed natural? We felt like celestial objects trailed by plumes of light. We spoke loudly, we told jokes. We made snide comments about the garbage, the pets, the children, the businesses, and each other, to prove we weren't complete idiots. Most of us were here because of failures elsewhere.

Actually, all of us were.

And we kept searching for her. We drove by the restaurant she was scheduled to renovate, and the boutique she had bulldozed. There were fuzzy Instagram photos of her in an orange hard hat—wasn't that her? We drove by the home of the family whose children she took to raise as her own. We snapped photos of the camera crew filming Main Street's shuttered buildings, the empty beer cans rolling down the street. We poked our iPhones out car windows and circled the hotel where she was staying, but most of us never even got a glimpse, and it frustrated us, it pained us; we pounded our fists on our steering wheels, and when we collided with each other we didn't laugh anymore, but punched each other in the face, and attracted police cars, and caused a scene—but not, usually, any cameras, and certainly not the Celebrity.

We skipped our sporadic jobs, and we locked our children out of the house, and when we passed each other on the pavement we didn't look up except to scowl and think: *You're not her.*

•

When the show aired two months later, the confidentiality agreements were voided, so we were free to talk about what had happened behind the scenes: how the Celebrity had torched the boutique's curtains and almost killed everyone; how she made the hotel staff cry and then hugged them and made them cry more; how the children had to be coaxed and bribed to object when they were taken from their parents and given to the Celebrity. How the dogs learned just enough history to form a small revolution and chase a gaffer onto a ledge.

We watched ourselves on TV walking down Main Street, talking about how much we hated this town and each other. We felt a strange compassion for ourselves, our voices and our images, and for our children, and our pets, and our old people.

For a while, we were grateful to the Celebrity for coming to town and making us famous, and then we were resentful, and then we forgot.

The show aired a few more episodes and then was canceled and then even the reruns were canceled. The mountain at the edge of town dissolved in the autumn rains. Some of us moved away from our town, but most of us stayed; some of us went to jail. Some of us started blogs, and two moved to California to study camera work and production design. One of us became a minor celebrity herself, and never came back to her hometown, and altered her IMDb bio to say she was from somewhere else.

Sometimes, we'd see a woman in a tattered white dress, or a man in a battered red bow tie, and we'd feel ashamed and confused, and not know why.

There are some of us who still remember, but it seems cruel to talk about—and even to think about—what it was like to be comets, trailed by lights and cameras and fuzzy microphones and kind voices telling us we were doing great, to just be ourselves.

Young Susan

On her fiftieth birthday, Susan bequeaths her old diaries to her children: James, twenty-five, and Kate, twenty-two. "Bequeath sounds like you're dead," says Kate. She takes the notebook-filled JC Penney bag between two fingers and drops it quickly beneath her chair. They are at Red Lobster, Susan's favorite restaurant, a place where they have celebrated graduations and birthdays and, once upon a time, anniversaries. And now: "You lucky kids! Kate, you get to read all about my college years, and my study abroad in London. And James, you get to read about my childhood and my twenties. Doesn't that sound interesting?"

Kate is staring down at her plate, at the boiled red creature that was so recently alive—was it recent? Or was it frozen and shipped from someplace far away after being plucked from the sea by an exploited child laborer? She heard something on the radio about this recently, but she can't remember the details. Just that the details are horrible. She brings a finger to her mouth and sucks, a habit from babyhood.

"Sure, Mom," says James in a voice pitched a little too high. He frowns down at his own Ann Taylor bag, then pulls out a green diary with a broken latch and opens it to a page of black crayon: *Mommy turned 30! We ate cake!*

His mother paws the diary out of his hands, saying, "This is from 1971. I was a very precocious child. *These* ones are from my early childhood, and these composition books are from the Tucson Years." She arches a brow. The Tucson Years are the years just before Susan met Kate and James' father.

She stopped keeping a journal after that. There was no point, really, as she'd learned. Your life just ceased to amaze. Or when it did amaze, words didn't suffice. She met Geoffrey; they moved to Maryland; they had kids. They got divorced. She dated a few men she could only describe as unexceptional—so why describe them at all? Over the years, she has considered destroying her journals, but this makes more sense. She will pass them along to her offspring: a record of their mother's madcap youth. Some of it really is madcap. She can hardly remember some of it.

"You can swap with each other when you're done," she says, dabbing her mouth with her napkin. She takes a sip of iced tea.

"I feel *very* uncomfortable," says Kate. "These are so personal."

"They're personal to young me, but old me wants you to have them." Susan realizes that both of her children have stopped eating. "I'm hoping you'll enjoy getting to know your young mom," she says. "I'm hoping you might learn something."

"Learn what?" asks James. He has stuffed the bag under the table and is ignoring his sister's heel digging into the side of his ankle.

"You tell me." Susan points at him with a bread stick. "You. Tell. Me."

•

When Kate was five, her favorite storybook was about a little bear that buried food in the dirt and then dug it up and fixed a meal for Mama and Papa Bear. There was probably more to it than that, but as Kate drives home in the October fog from her mother's birthday lunch, back to the Annapolis house she shares with two roommates—one she made the mistake of sleeping with last week—she is thinking of that story, and of her five-year-old self going through the refrigerator looking for food to bury. She thinks of her brother saying, "You're going to get in trouble," as she carried a packet of ground beef, a carrot, and a foil-wrapped block of Velveeta into the backyard. She dug the hole with her sandbox shovel, unwrapped the meat and cheese, and placed the food in the ground.

It was immensely satisfying, filling that hole in the ground with food and then dirt, and it was satisfying even after James tattled, after the spanking, after the lecture about food being too expensive to waste. It was, she thinks now, the first truly creative gesture of her life, even if she did get the idea from a book. She works as a receptionist at an optometrist's office, but her degree is in art history. Her last girlfriend took photographs of abandoned buildings, then set the photos on fire and took pictures of the photo-fires and sold those photos in Boston galleries for hundreds of dollars. Maybe Kate should take a picture of her mother's journals covered in dirt; maybe it's enough just to dig a hole and throw them in.

•

"What are you doing out here?" Samantha asks her a half hour later as Kate shovels in the drizzle next to the withered tomato garden. This is Samantha's house; or rather, her parents' house. They bought it for her and told her she could rent it out as long as she was responsible and didn't trash the place or grow pot in the basement. They said they trusted her judgement in terms of roommates. And now here's Kate—lovely, lovely Kate, who Samantha suspects

might have been at least slightly high when they had sex
last week—sweating like a madwoman and digging up the
yard.

"Nothing to worry about," Kate calls, not looking up.
"I'll fill the hole in, I promise. I'm just burying some stuff."

Samantha tells herself she will dig it up later—whatever it is—but somehow she never does. She and Kate will
never sleep together again, and two months later, Kate will
inform her that she's moving to Orlando. In April, Samantha's father will have the first of three heart attacks; her
mother will sign the paperwork to sell the house; and after
her father's death, Samantha will move back to her childhood home by the Chesapeake Bay.

The Annapolis house will be demolished to make room
for a politician's mansion. Seventeen months after Kate
buries the journals in the backyard, a backhoe operator will
dig up the plastic JC Penney bag, notebooks spilling out,
and it will occur to him that he should have been much,
much more careful when he disposed of the remains of the
girl he killed four months earlier, the girl who rests now in
his own backyard, swaddled in Hefty bags, deep beneath
his wife's marigolds.

He will stop the backhoe, leap out of the cab. Once, long
ago, he backhoed a nest of hissing copperheads from a
house high in the Phoenix foothills; they hissed and flailed
and almost fell right into his lap. But this bag contains not
snakes, not body parts, not treasure: just notebooks, who
cares, one with LONDON 1987 scrawled across it.

If, in some other permutation of events and impulses,
he brings this bag home, if he leaves the seven journals
on the kitchen table, his son—fifteen, shy, friendless, and
imaginative—will be moved to read them. He will page
through Young Susan's adventures; he will acquire a crush
on Young Susan, walking through Hampstead Heath in her
black boots, Young Susan with her Silk Cut cigarettes and
her Jack Kerouac obsession. And, when he's nineteen, he
will find himself at The World's End pub in Camden Town,

drinking a pint of Young Susan's favorite beer—Harp—and thus begin a long, long process of putting the past behind him and moving on, in a place where no one knows what his father had done, or what his mother had done to his father.

The backhoe operator, however, will not be moved to take the journals home; he will jump back into the cab and continue to haul the dirt, extracting the bones of pets and mice, lost earrings and old shoes, oyster shells, igneous and sedimentary rocks, twenty-four glass beads and a fossilized shark tooth.

•

James' girlfriend Mags has not yet told him she's pregnant when he comes home from his mother's fiftieth birthday lunch looking weary and strange. It's a week before Halloween, and she should be making decorations for her third graders: pumpkins and spiders, sugar cookies with orange icing. But she hasn't felt like making cookies or decorations; she's been cranky and bloated and gassy.

"My mother is a lunatic," James says as he sinks into a kitchen chair.

It's Sunday, but they never go to church. Will they have to go to church when the baby comes? Is that how life works? It's occurred to her that she doesn't know how most of life works. She's twenty-four years old and she met James at the Middleton Tavern two years ago, a drunken hookup that stuck. James is holding out an Ann Taylor bag, and she says, "Ooh, what'd you get me?"

He dumps out a pile of pastel children's diaries and black composition books. "This," he says, "is my mother's youth." He grimaces. "I'm supposed to read them to get to know her."

"Oh, no," says Mags. She feels the urge to comfort him, but she's not sure if comfort is required in this kind of situation.

"My mother's youth," James repeats glumly. He's thinking that he and Mags should move, maybe to Boston or
Philadelphia, maybe get married. He has a degree in biology but works as the manager of a bulk candy store by the
harbor. He's thinking that he must be a terrible son not to
want to know about his mother's youth.

Mags has opened one of the pastel diaries. "*Today we
learned about sea horses. John W. smells like bacon,* with four
exclamation points. Huh," she says, and picks up a composition book. "This looks like drunken handwriting, but
I think these are sketches of cactus. At least, I hope that's
cactus." She sniffs the pages, wrinkles her nose. "Did your
mother *smoke*?"

"No," he says, and then he remembers that yes, she did.
He remembers his young mother smoking outside in the
cold air, the steam from her breath and the smoke mingling
and rising into the antlered trees. His father calling for her
to come inside.

James has never understood the need for journals;
he started a WordPress blog a few years ago, *Observations of People,* but he lost interest in people and now can't
remember his password. He played guitar in a band in
high school, and he's experimented with writing his own
songs—most recently a country-twangy number called
"Green-Eyed Girl," which is about Mags and which he's
been embarrassed to play for her. But he will play it later
this evening after she tells him about the baby, and he will
be inspired throughout her pregnancy to write more songs,
for her and for the new baby, a girl who will grow up to
have no interest in her father's original compositions that
he will try to foist upon her on her sixteenth birthday.

It will be another two weeks before they tell anyone
else about the pregnancy. They will invite Kate and Susan
over for dinner, and halfway through the taco salad the
neighbor's sister will pop over to ask if anyone has jumper
cables—sorry to disturb! Oh, but she will be delightful.
Kate, especially, will be delighted. They've all (except for

Mags) had too much wine, and they offer the woman some wine, and she tells them she lives in Orlando and works at Epcot Center, folding wool sweaters in fake England.

She has a fabulous fake British accent, and Susan laughs and tries out her own fake accent, but she doesn't mention her study abroad, and she doesn't ask about the diaries because she's realized that bequeathing them was a terrible idea. She would not be dismayed to know that Kate buried them; she would not mind that James has stuffed his bag in the closet without looking at them. In those closet-hidden journals, which her children will not read and her granddaughter will not read, either, Young Susan, back from England and missing the cold and the fog and the damp cobblestones, stamps angrily through the Tucson sunlight. She drives her Plymouth Sundance into the foothills, and she smokes moody cigarettes and blows smoke out over the saguaros. She sketches cactus and sometimes goes to a bar called the Shanty and writes descriptions of the people there, just observations of people, and then she drives home and falls into her futon and sleeps and sleeps, and wakes to go to her temp job at the university, and wonders if her life will ever get interesting, not yet understanding that it already is.

Susan has considered asking for the journals back, but that's not what she wants, either. Mostly she wants the past to be something that doesn't hover like a ghost but rather something like legs, moving you forward without you giving it too much thought.

James' girlfriend has been sipping soda water all evening. Outside, the yellow-red trees glow in the porch light; the moon is fogged and the air smells of distant bonfires. Susan thinks of Tucson, the mesquite smoke in the air, the woman selling tamales outside of the Safeway at Campbell and Broadway. She never wrote any of this down, but there it is. No, thank you, she said to the tamale woman every time.

"So hey," says Mags. "I have something important to say."

Susan was about to tell them about the woman selling tamales, how she wishes she'd bought one, just once, but now doesn't seem like the time. James is red-cheeked and smiling, gazing at Mags; Kate and the fake-Brit are laughing, heads tilted together. No one has looked for jumper cables. If she still kept a journal, she might try to write about the foggy moonlight or the smell of distant bonfires, or the way Mags glows as she rises from the table, holding her goblet of ice water like a chalice. Or she might get distracted by the past, as so often happens these days, and write about the tamale woman, or the time she lost little James at the shopping mall, or Kate crying when the dog ate her Cabbage Patch doll. Or she might write about something lovely, like splashing through the Paris rain with her husband when everything was still so good. It's all still in there somewhere, she marvels, as Mags clangs her fork on her glass for attention, and all eyes turn to her.

Hi Ho Cherry-O

I've just asked Wendell to access data pertaining to twentieth-century board games when he says, "Tie me up and leave me in the closet for an hour."

"Excuse me?" I say. Wendell has been my research assistant for six months. He lives with my husband and me, has his own workspace in a corner of the dining room. He's a new brand of Service Robot my university recently acquired. He accesses other remote robots to help me retrieve data. He's bright red, about four feet tall, and has a head that looks like two old-fashioned blow dryers put side-by-side. He has round green eyes that blink. Until now, he hasn't said anything more to me than, "Right away," or "You bet."

"Ha, ha," I say, because I'm guessing this is a joke. Not that I've ever heard him joke.

"There's twine in the kitchen drawer," Wendell says. He has an Australian accent, but I could have made him sound French or Irish, or like a small Cockney child. "Tie me up and leave me in the closet for an hour, and then I'll access that data."

"I can't do that," I tell him. "Seriously."

He doesn't say anything. I ask him again about his board game data, and he still doesn't say anything. "Are you okay, Wendell?" I ask.

"There's twine in the kitchen drawer," Wendell repeats. "Tie me up and leave me in the closet for an hour, and then I'll access that data." He sounds so cheerful and sure of himself.

So I do it. I feel a little bit weird, but maybe it has something to do with his electrical system. I figure Wendell knows what's best for himself. I don't really know how these robots work. I'm more of a historian. When I take him out of the closet an hour later and untie him, he says, "I've sent that data to your workstation," and I say, "Thanks, Wendell."

When my husband gets home from work, I tell him about Wendell asking me to tie him up. He looks horrified. "You didn't, did you?"

"Of course not," I lie. "But—he's a robot. He—*it*—can't feel. It's just programmed that way." This is what I told myself as I wrapped the twine around his metal body and rolled him into the closet.

"You should get a replacement."

"But Wendell's already downloaded so much already. It's too much trouble to find someone new at this point."

My husband says, "Well, keep an eye on him. It could be some kind of malfunction."

"Oh, I will," I tell him.

•

The next day, Wendell rolls into my office and starts working right away. He's found commercials of children playing games called Lite-Brite and Chutes and Ladders and Hi Ho! Cherry-O. The children in these commercials are very white and dimpled and mostly wear stripes, and they shout a lot. They are very, very happy children. My research involves childhood in the twentieth century, which even though it wasn't that long ago is difficult because so much was deleted or destroyed in fires and floods. I've done some interviews at old folks' homes. I've done some memory scans. What's confusing is that most of what Wendell is finding doesn't necessarily corroborate the memory scans.

My husband works as a counselor at a Home for the Disembodied, so he can commute remotely from the Virtual station in our bedroom. We've talked about getting a larger apartment, but this works for now. He stays in the bedroom and I stay out here with Wendell, and then we have dinner together.

I thank Wendell for finding those commercials, but when I ask if he's found anything about something called Battleship (which came up in the memory scans), he says, "I believe I can find that information. But first, scrape me with a knife hard enough to leave a mark."

"I can't damage you," I tell him. "I won't get my deposit back."

"Then put your hands around my neck and squeeze as hard as you can."

He waits. I wait. I say, "Who programmed you?"

"I'm programmed to work for you," he says in his cheerful Australian accent. "I am at your disposal. I am here to assist with your research. This will be easier if you do what I ask."

So I do. When he says, "You're not squeezing as hard as you can," I squeeze harder. He doesn't so much have a neck as a plastic cylinder but I feel it getting warmer as I squeeze and when he says, "Okay, that was great, you can stop now," I keep squeezing a little bit longer.

•

At dinner, my husband starts to say something but stops himself. I know this is because his other family came to visit him at the Home for the Disembodied. He has a wife who's an actress and triplet sons, aged seven. They're always aged seven, which he says he finds somewhat frustrating—how there's only so much you can do with them, how you can never hope they'll turn out to be more than they are. But then he has the opposite problem with his actress-wife, whom he doesn't recognize from day to day. Finally, I told him I was sick of hearing about his other family. Even though he explained that he was with them because he felt sorry for them, and that he and the actress-wife hardly ever had sex anymore, we agreed not to speak of them.

"Well, what is it?" I ask at last. "Go ahead and tell me."

"I know you don't like to hear about them," he says, but I make a rollie-motion with my hand that is meant to convey *get on with it*. "The triplets and I shot some hoops is all," he says. "And they were good. And they got better as they played. It was something." He forks some pasta into his mouth. "I think I can maybe get them on a team," he says, his mouth full and muffled. "Coach them."

"Huh," I say.

"How was your day?" he asks.

"It was the usual," I tell him.

•

My husband and I have talked about having children, either virtual or real. We have polite, reasonable conversations about how we should have sex again sometime, but then we just crawl into bed and lie next to each other until we fall asleep. But maybe someday, when we're sixty, we might try for a child. Except the world is getting smaller. Most things disappear: cities, glaciers, mountains, civilizations. I don't want to raise children in a Home for the Disembodied. I want them here, in the flesh, but my husband says that's too dangerous, he doesn't have the stomach for it. I wonder if he would feel differently if we could produce dimpled, stripes-wearing children who roll dice and make cakes in plastic ovens and rejoice when plastic cherries fill up their little buckets.

●

The next morning, Wendell isn't at his workstation. I drink coffee, go through my documents and my video streams and the transcripts of the memory scans. Some of the memory scan interviewees end up in a Home for the Disembodied, but it's impossible to interview them there because all they want to talk about is tennis and sex, and most of them don't even remember their previous embodied lives.

Finally, I say, "Wendell?" and find him behind the laundry room door. He doesn't answer. "Are you not feeling well?" I ask. "Did you find anything about Battleship?"

He raises his blow dryer head and says, "I'm not feeling motivated."

"Well," I say. "What would motivate you?"

"Tell me you hate me because I'm stupid. Tell me I should drown myself in a toxic lake."

"Well," I say. "But I don't hate you. I actually appreciate your help. You're a good worker."

He doesn't say anything. I go back to work reading the memory scans, but I can't find anything about Battleship, or about something called a Donny and Marie lunchbox, or about something called Free Parking that led to broken friendships among the interviewees: *I told Krista that you got five hundred bucks when you landed on Free Parking, and she said you didn't, and we never spoke again after that day.* It's so goddamn frustrating. Wendell has access to other Service Robots all over the world and all he has to do is ask them, and they'll tell him everything I want to know.

I go back to Wendell, who hasn't moved. "You're supposed to be programmed to help me," I say. "So help me!"

"But first, put a plastic bag over my head and secure it with a large rubber band that you can find in your desk."

So I do it. He looks helpless and ridiculous and terrifying. The plastic bag is white and makes him look like a robot ghost. He says, "Now tell me you hate me because I'm stupid and you want me to drown in a toxic lake."

"I hate you," I tell him, "you goddamn piece of shit, because you're stupid, and you should drown yourself in a toxic lake."

"Thanks!" he says cheerfully, and the printer starts whirring and my computer lights up with the sound of music and children laughing and singing.

He doesn't ask me to take the plastic bag off, so I just leave it there.

•

When I told my dissertation director what I wanted to write about, she looked dismayed and said, "Oh, that's pretty bold of you." What she meant was: Who wants to be reminded of what we can't get back? What good will that do? She said, "I would like to caution you against it." Then she leaned back in her big chair and said, "What was your childhood like?"

That was a very personal question coming from her. I said, "I had the same childhood as everybody, with my screens and my worlds and all that." I didn't tell her that I was raised in an orphanage because my parents lived at a Home for the Disembodied. But they did their best. They taught me how to do puzzles and fly a virtual plane and how to do very complicated math, and they eventually deleted themselves when they said the world scared them too much.

"I'll sign off on this," she said, signing off on it. "But I think you'll find that whatever you're looking for isn't there."

"I'm not looking for anything," I told her.

"It won't add up," she said, and I said, "It doesn't have to," because I had no idea what she meant.

But now I'm starting to understand. She checked in with me last week to let me know that my dissertation was almost a month late, and if I ever wanted to finish and get on with my life, I should submit it to the department. "Okay," I said.

It occurred to me for the first time that she and I never discussed what getting on with my life might mean.

•

I call the university and ask if it might be possible to exchange Wendell for another Service Robot and they say are you kidding? Are you insane? That robot was programmed to make your life easier.

"Oh, great, thanks," I say.

This morning, Wendell isn't in his corner. He's not in the closet or the bathroom or behind the laundry room door or in my office, so that means there's only one place left to look, and sure enough there he is in the bedroom. He's standing about a foot from my husband, who is sitting at his workstation, the top half of his body swallowed by the VR unit. He's lost in his Disembodied world, counseling newbies, leading discussions, giving tennis lessons, coaching the triplets, and hardly ever having sex with his actress-wife.

"I found some information about Battleship," Wendell says. He still has the bag on his head. I feel like everyone is underwater but me.

I'm rarely this close to my husband while he's at work. I know he can't hear or see me; he's in his world and I'm in this one. "I also found out about Rock 'Em Sock 'Em and music that makes you dance and dance."

I want to know about these things.

Then he just stops talking.

"What do you need me to do?" I ask, but he doesn't answer. "You're a stupid piece of shit," I say, hopefully. "You're just a piece of metal with no soul. You're not real." Nothing. "I don't know what you want from me," I say.

I take a pair of metal nail clippers and scrape along the side of his body, leaving a long white mark. I'll lose my deposit, but to hell with it. I write IDIOT on him in permanent marker. This doesn't seem like enough. I pull the bag off his head and his glowing green eyes stare, blink. I slap him across his head. I slap him again. It's a game, I tell myself, like happy children used to play. Just figure out the rules.

He doesn't say anything.

I go into the kitchen and turn the kettle on. When it whistles, I carry it into the bedroom and pour boiling water over Wendell's head; steam rises all around us, and hot water soaks the carpet. From inside his VR unit, my husband lets out a long sigh.

Wendell says, "Battleship was a guessing game, thought to have its origins before World War I. It's a game of strategy. In 1967, Milton Bradley produced a plastic version. The game was played on grids. The goal was to sink your opponent's ship." And he flashes a commercial on the wall of the bedroom, two little boys sitting by a lake, one saying, "J1!" and the other saying, "You sank my battleship!" and falling backward into the water while the other boy laughs.

"I don't understand this," I say. I stomp my feet, and I wonder if my husband's world is shaking somewhere, if maybe one of the triplets missed making a basket. "And I still need to know about Free Parking. What the fuck is that?"

But Wendell goes quiet again, and after I slap him a few more times and knock him over and call him a piece of trash I know we're done for the day, so I put him in the closet with the old computers and the vacuum cleaner. I take a deep breath. Something is happening, a feeling like when my parents taught me math problems and finally, finally, I could solve them.

At dinner, my husband compliments the pasta and asks me how my day was.

"It was great," I tell him, because I have realized this is true.

He says, "You seem like you're in a good mood!" and I say, "I am." My heart is beating so hard that I can hardly eat. I say, "Tell me about your day, honey."

He stares at me, fork suspended.

"Really," I say. "Honey, sweetheart, love." And I sit back while he tells me—first nervously, then with enthusiasm—about the triplets playing basketball, and about his wife's new red hair, and how he's trying out for a play they're putting on at the Home for the Disembodied, so he might be home late some nights. "That's really, really great," I say, because I'm happy for him, and for me, making such progress, finally.

And later, when we get into bed, I crawl on top of him—how long has it been?—and press a gentle, gentle finger over his lips, his neck. "What?" he says, his eyes wide. My blood is rising, my fingers are tingling, my husband's pulse a sparrow beneath my hands. "Oh, no, I don't think so," he says and rolls over. "Is that okay?" he asks, his back hunched toward me.

"Of course," I tell him. "It's fine." I stare at the ceiling. My husband's breathing turns to snores. "It's fine," I say again. And what I'm thinking is that tomorrow I will ask Wendell more questions, knowing that all the answers will confuse and infuriate me. When he goes silent I will pound his head into the wall, hard enough to leave a dent; I will wrap him in plastic; freeze him in ice, burn him, call him terrible, terrible things—whatever it takes until he throws all his cherries in the air and tells me I've won.

Sea Ice

The disgraced professor entered the college cafeteria. She held her head high, looking straight ahead. Of course she could hear the students whispering. Of course she could see her colleagues turning away. It was Titanic night, the tables set with white tablecloths, the chafing dishes heating up replicas of the passengers' last meal, as reinterpreted by the Mennonite cafeteria staff: green peas, chicken Kiev, roast beef, sautéed potatoes. Éclairs for dessert.

The line started at the double doors of the cafeteria; everybody loved Titanic night. The professors came with their spouses. The students were dressed up in suits or gowns; some of the boys wore top hats. Where did a college student in rural Pennsylvania get a top hat? The student workers wore black and white, like servants in Downton Abbey.

The professor shuffled her way through the line. No one spoke to her. Her hair was in a ponytail, and she could almost pass as a student, even though she was twenty years older than the students. But she could still get away with bangs. She was wearing a light green rain jacket and blue jeans. She picked up a tray, a white plate, knife, fork, spoon. She said hello to the student workers behind their silver serving trays, and some of them said: "Hello,

Dr. D," but they couldn't look her in the eye. She said: "Oh, yummy." She said: "I look forward to this every year."

She walked straight-backed with her tray through the cafeteria, the round tables set with baskets of linen-swaddled dinner rolls and sweating goblets of water, the lemons floating like doomed life rafts. She found an empty table by the dish room. No one sat with her. She ignored the stares, the glares, the cleared throats. She ate quickly, took her tray to the dish room window, and left.

Outside, in the dark April night, rain clouds gathered, lightning flashed; inside, the electricity flickered. "We've hit an iceberg," said somebody. Outside, the professor pulled up her hood. She'd forgotten an umbrella, left it back in her office, the scene of the crime that wasn't a crime. She ducked her head against the rain and ran.

•

My name is Margaret, and I'm the one Dr. D left to die outside her office reading text alerts of an active (but ultimately non-existent) shooter making his way through the building. I'm the one who knocked on her office door and said, "Can I please come in so I don't die?" The one who begged: "Please?" And she said nothing. That was a week ago, and I got an extension on all of my assignments because I would have been dead if there actually had been a shooter, which there wasn't.

I'm standing at my station tong-ing out crab legs—there weren't crab legs on the Titanic, but we have them at every fancy dinner at this college. Dr. D steered clear of me, but the other professors go out of their way to say hello—they all suddenly know my name. They say, "How are you *doing*, Margaret?" and I hold up my silver tongs and say, "Would you care for some crab legs?"

A bald history professor in an ascot says, "Nice legs!" and then, realizing how pervy that sounded, gasps, "I'm so sorry," and scuttles off, legless. You can't be too careful.

My roommate Tara comes through the line, and I give her three crab legs even though we're just supposed to give out two. She's wearing the black dress she wore to her father's funeral. "Did you *see* her?" she asks. "Can you believe the nerve?" Tara has been very vocal on my behalf; she started a petition to get Dr. D fired, even though I didn't ask her to. I don't know what I want to happen. There's a part of me that feels like a ghost, and another part of me that doesn't.

"It's fine," I say to Tara, who shakes her head as she moves down the line toward the roast beef.

At seven-fifteen, my boyfriend, Curt, comes in with his roommate, Craig. Curt and Craig: that sounds like two jocks even though they're stoners, not jocks. They sit cross-legged across from each other on their beds and clip their big yellow toenails.

They're drenched from the rain, wearing handmade Grateful Dead shirts. Since the crab legs are long gone, I've been reassigned to peas. "Give peas a chance," says Craig, and Curt laughs like that's so original.

"With the melting sea ice," says Curt, "the Titanic would be fine. Like, global warming would help it."

Tara swoops by on her way out the door, trailed by a freshman dude, Thor, who is very small for his name. "Are you okay, sweetie?" she says to me. "Dr. D was here," she explains to Curt and Craig, and makes her eyes go wide. "Can you believe the nerve?"

"Why is she still here?" says Curt. "Hashtag fire the bitch."

"I'm fine!" I say. "Seriously, it's fine."

The cafeteria is clearing out. Curt and Craig do a quick loop, then wave goodbye and head out the doors, their pockets stuffed with dinner rolls. The full-time staff is pacing, restless, ready to put up the chairs and mop the floor and go home to wherever they live. This is a small town, halfway between Hershey Park and Harrisburg. In a year I will graduate and begin the quest to pay off my student loans with my English degree. I will launch myself into the world, whatever that means, as they keep telling us in the English Capstone class, the one that Dr. D used to teach, about how to find jobs and get letters of rec. Another professor is taking the class over for the last three weeks of the semester.

At exactly eight p.m., "Nearer My God to Thee" comes over the loudspeaker, and that's the cue for everyone to grab that last éclair and go. I turn in my apron, grab my coat, and step out into the night, feeling the sharp air on my skin, smelling like the crabby sea.

•

Dr. D on her first day fifteen years ago: hair a sliced angle on one side, buzz cut on the other. Her colleagues were giddy. Their new hire was so young, so hip!

"Hip is out," said someone. "No one says hip."

"I need a new hip," said someone else.

Dr. Frame said: "Oh, how I wish I could still wear high heels. But my arches just cramp up!"

Dr. D wore short, swishy skirts and high, strappy heels. "Call me Debbie!" said Dr. D to her students, but they couldn't call her Debbie, no way. They were eighteen years old, from rural Pennsylvania, and they didn't call their teachers by their first names, so they called her nothing. But they admired her crazy haircut and how she would stop in the middle of her lecture on *Jane Eyre* to say, "That Rochester is a creep, who's with me?" and how she wrote friendly comments on all of their papers, didn't just slap a grade on them.

Was she single, married? All signs pointed to single. Which meant a boyfriend? Or—glory be—a girlfriend? She made tantalizing comments about her "ex," whom she left behind in Tennessee. Her accent was Southern but not *too* Southern; she sounded like a country singer, but not like a hick. She decorated her office with pictures of pastel alleyways and green mountains. "San Miguel de Allende, Mexico," she'd say when anyone asked. "Study abroad changed my life! Have you considered it? You should do it!"

In early December of her first semester, the snow began to fall at three a.m., and by seven the campus was covered in white. The snow kept falling; classes weren't canceled, because this was Pennsylvania and everyone lived on campus, so students crunched and slid and skated to their classes, and Dr. D said, peering out the window of her third floor classroom, "It's like a Bruegel painting down there!" Her cheeks were flushed. No one knew what the hell she was talking about. Later, she flopped herself down in the middle of the quad and made snow angels, which filled again with snow.

•

My dorm room smells like weed and rotten fruit and incense, which means Tara has been hanging out with Shannon from down the hall—Shannon with her apple bongs and record collection on actual vinyl, which she can't do anything with because nobody has a record player. Tara is sitting at her desk, which is unusual, and the room is dark except for her laptop and her desk light. The dorm was built in the 1930s, and I wonder, as I do occasionally, who lived in this room back when there were typewriters and you could still smoke cigarettes and listen to records on a record player. I wonder how many of the girls who lived in this room are now dead, which is a thing I didn't wonder a week ago. But there must be quite a few.

"You're going to get caught if you keep apple-bonging in here," I say, even though Shannon is the RA and she's the only one who could catch us.

"Tell me what you think of this," Tara says. "Dear President Henderson, we hereby declare a walkout at eleven a.m. on Monday, April 19, to protest the continued employment of Dr. Debra Duggar, a coward and a traitor."

"Wow," is all I can think to say. I flip on the overhead light so I can see what I'm doing in the closet. I pull off my server skirt and blouse and hang them up, even though they smell, and change into sweats. My phone dings with a text from Curt: *Coming over?* I text, *Gotta study*, and he texts a poo. Ours is not a great love story. Ours is a story of boredom and horniness. Now that I'm not-dead, I have seriously considered whether there's any reason to keep hanging out with him, and I've come to the conclusion that there's still no real reason not to. And this makes me feel disappointed in myself.

"If the walkout is at eleven," says Tara, "then I won't have to take that world history test."

"You'll have to take it eventually," I say. "But I really don't want a walkout."

"It's not for *you*," she says. "This is bigger than you now."

That's what I was afraid she'd say.

•

Twenty-year-old Debbie, walking down the sun-spackled streets of San Miguel de Allende, doing tequila shots with her classmates, making out with that guy, what's-his-name. What was his name? It didn't matter. During the day she strolled with her study abroad group through the pastel streets and took notes on the architecture, the history, the art! At night: tequila and foolishness, and let's walk to that cemetery past the plaza, the one with all the bones just lying there, just out in the open. Twenty-year-old Debbie, walking over the bones of the dead, picking up a bone, a sliver—a finger?—and putting it in her pocket, her heart thudding. Was this against the law? Against some law? Against all the laws? She had a human bone in her pocket, and she was walking through the dark streets with a group of laughing girls who also had bones in their pockets. Bone Girls, she thought, and shuddered with terror and joy.

Later, back home in Memphis for Christmas break, she would take the bone from her box of souvenirs and think: Who *were* you? She didn't believe in random curses, but she believed that you could disturb the dead and knock something in the shadow-world off-kilter, which was worse than curses. Twenty-year-old Debbie ran outside in the December chill, into the woods behind her house, her house churning out chimney smoke from the fireplace, her mother inside angry with her brother, her father locked away behind his office door writing sermons. She took the bone from her pocket and threw it into the trees.

•

My parents drive sixty miles up from Maryland and take me to the one good restaurant in town, the one with dim lighting and wooden tables and candles. It's supposed to be German, which means the waitresses have to wear demeaning dirndls and everything comes with potatoes. My father gallantly pulls out my mother's chair, and then mine, and then my mother bursts into tears.

"We should have come sooner," she says. "You look terrible."

"I'm fine," I say. I'm a little bit high. My eyes feel like squirrel's eyes. I realize I haven't eaten in a while, because the smell of sauerkraut actually makes me hungry. "Things are good," I hear myself saying. "I got extensions on all of my assignments." It occurs to me that the extensions were for a week, and a week has already passed. Or more than a week. Who can tell anymore? I've had one session with the school counselor, who told me it was normal to feel the way I was feeling, even though I didn't tell him how I was feeling because I didn't even know.

My father says, "We want you home this summer. No more working on campus. You can help your mother at the store. Or take violin lessons." My mother owns a popcorn store and needs no help, and I have never mentioned any desire to play violin. My father is an accountant in Balti-more and tried to talk me into being an accounting major, and now I'm not sure what he's trying to talk me into.

We order pork chops and potatoes and sauerkraut, and I don't just eat my food but devour it. I pick up the chop with my fingers and gnaw and feel like making ani-mal noises. I am a body without a soul, or a soul without a body. Sometimes when I walk past Howard Hall, where I thought I was going to die, I see myself staring out the windows.

"So listen," my mother says. Her face is bright in the candlelight. The dirndl waitress has poured all of us more iced tea. "We're suing that woman for pain and suffering. And we hope you'll go to the walkout."

"You are?" I say. "And about the walkout: I mean, I don't even have a class then, so there's nothing for me to walk out of."

"People are coming all the way from Harrisburg," my father says.

"All the way from Philly," my mother says.

"People are driving here for the walkout?" I start laugh-ing and can't stop so I drink down all my iced tea until my chest feels frozen. As we're leaving the restaurant, some of the other diners turn and applaud.

•

After seven years at the college, Dr. D earned a sabbatical and boy did she need it. She went to the South of France to write poems about art, although she made it sound much more impressive in her sabbatical application. She mentioned the word *ekphrasis* seven times and referenced Cézanne and Zola and cross-cultural experience. She didn't mention the handsome art teacher she'd met at a conference in Chicago. She moved into his sprawling house in Aix-en-Provence and drank too much red wine every night. Her poems were shockingly sexual, and she submitted them to literary journals whose editors were shocked enough to publish them. She spent the autumn walking under golden trees on the Cours Mirabeau and driving with the art teacher to small villages in the Luberon Valley, and she started and abandoned two novels: one shockingly sexual, one from the point of view of a dog.

She did not mention, in her post-sabbatical narrative, that the art teacher was married or that his wife arrived from Chicago to find her, Dr. D, drunk on the terrace; she didn't mention the shattering wine glasses, or the small hotel she moved into for the remaining weeks of her stay. She didn't try to write a poem about this, because it was both too traumatizing and too much of a cliché. Why did life have to break your heart in such predictable ways? Or maybe that was the point of art: to render the cliché of human experience in a way that didn't feel like a cliché? Well, good luck with that.

There are former students out there in the world who still remember what happened the spring semester after her return: how she once ran out of the classroom in tears, how she told a girl her poem was "better off as a paper airplane," how she could be seen plunging blindly into the street, as if she were *trying* to get hit by a car. *What's up with Dr. D?* the students wondered—but only briefly. In late March, she flew home to Tennessee for her mother's funeral, and her classes signed a sympathy card for her. She returned clear-eyed and wearing an engagement ring. She never spoke of her fiancé. By May, the ring was gone.

She held her usual end-of-semester salon at her red brick house on College Avenue, and the students sat in a circle in her living room, under Cézanne prints, and read their poems in trembling voices. When they were done, Dr. D smiled and murmured something that sounded like, "You're all fools," or "You're all so cool," and no one asked her to repeat herself. Better not to know.

●

On Saturday morning, Dr. Frame tweets out a long thread about how faculty are meant to protect their students, how they are charged with preserving young lives, then keels over dead of a heart attack.

Later that afternoon, the editor of the school newspaper shows up in my dorm room. I've been deleting her emails for days: *We're going to run the story, and we'd love to have your point of view!!!! Did you know that Dr. D is taking a leave of absence? How do you feel about that?? Do you want her fired? Will you participate in the walkout? Did she even apologize???*

But now here she is, this newspaper editor with her little-girl braids and big glasses, flapping her steno pad at me. I wish I could delete her from my room, but she's somehow pushed her way inside and is now sitting at Tara's desk. "My roommate will be back soon, and she needs to sit there," is all I can think to say. But Tara's been spending all her time with young Thor.

"First of all," she says, her eyes tiny behind her big glasses, "how *are* you? How are you *doing?*"

I'm still in my sweats at five p.m., and I haven't showered in days. I wonder if this is how Jesus felt in his tomb, festering in his own funk, wondering when he could get on with his life. This is an odd thing for me to wonder, since I'm not religious, but lately strange thoughts occur to me. Last night I dreamed I was a vampire, and the first person I killed was the newspaper editor, but I don't tell her this.

"I'm fine," I say.

"Did she even apologize? Like, after it happened?"

"Did you talk to her?" I haven't seen her since Titanic night, and I wonder if anybody else has.

"No, unfortunately. She won't answer my emails. I went to her house and she wouldn't open the door—but her car was there! But what would *you* tell her, if you could?" She holds her pen above her notepad.

"I'd tell her the school newspaper editor is stalking her."

She pouts. Slaps her notebook shut and stands. "I'm just trying to give you a *voice*," she says. "But if you're one of those women who doesn't believe in speaking her truth, there's nothing I can do about it." Then her eyes soften. "I'll write that you're still in shock, still processing the trauma. I'll say you look like a person trapped between life and death."

"Fuck off," I tell her.

•

Last October, six months before the shooter-that-wasn't, Dr. D found herself in the one good restaurant in town with her newly-divorced, shitfaced brother, visiting from Memphis. Was she also shitfaced? Probably so. A former student whose name Dr. D couldn't remember served them big German beers. The girl had graduated—when? Last year? Two years ago? And now she was wearing a demeaning dirndl and saying, "Can I interest you in some schnitzel?"

"No, thank you," said Dr. D, and her brother held up his stein and said, "Keep these coming, honey."

The restaurant was dim and quiet on a Thursday night; outside, dead leaves spiraled to the ground under the streetlights. The townies had decorated their porches with grinning pumpkins and plastic spiders. Dr. D had decorated her own porch with an altar featuring three plastic skeletons wearing lipstick, wreathed in flowers, all of them missing one finger bone.

"How can you live in this place, Debs?" her brother asked. "It's like Bumfuck, Egypt. Except it's not like Egypt at all, because everybody's fat and white." He pouted into his beer. "Do you know that waitress? Tell her she'll get extra credit if she brings more big beers right now."

The waitress—what the hell was her name?—had wandered off and was staring at the big wooden front doors as if expecting them to blow open and whisk her into some other life. *Mr. Rochester isn't so bad,* Dr. D suddenly remembered her saying from the back of the class. *He just has low self-esteem.*

"She already graduated," Dr. D said. In a low voice, she added, "She was sweet but dumb." Oh dear. Was that mean? She didn't mean to be mean.

Her brother was waving the waitress over; there seemed to be two of her. Dr. D closed one eye and then there was one of her.

Her brother leaned forward and gave a tiny belch. "My sister says you're sweet but dumb. Is that true?"

The girl (Kaitlin? Kaley? Karlee?) seemed to stop breathing. Her mouth opened, then shut. Later, Dr. D would write a poem about her, and in the poem the girl clawed off the demeaning dirndl and stomped off into the night; she went to the South of France and was never heard of again. Dr. D would do forty-seven drafts of this poem, two of which would be sestinas, and then burn them all in her fireplace.

"Can we get our check, please?" Dr. D asked gently.

"Of course," said the girl, teeth bared and white. Animal teeth. This would also go in Dr. D's poem. "You got it."

•

On Sunday morning, I'm woken by a dragon breathing and look outside to see a hot air balloon rising on the quad. It's secured by long yellow ropes, so it doesn't get far, but I have the strange idea that it's there for me, that I'm meant to board it and float, Dorothy-like, into another world. The balloon is green and blue and filled with fire. The sun shines down on students playing Frisbee on the lawn.

I picture an imaginary girl standing here years from now, thinking about how I used to live in this room, before my tragic death caused by Dr. D not saving me. It's my nonexistent future, the one where, because I died tragically, I could have been anything: a politician, an artist, an astronaut! But none of this is true, and I think this is what people are really mad about, even if they can't admit it.

But I try to feel like that fire-breathing balloon, so I rise and float out into the hallway, into the smell of shower soap and sour beer, Shannon the RA saluting me as she strides by with her shower bucket. She skids to a halt and pivots. "You going to the service?" she says.

"What service?"

"Memorial service for Dr. Frame. At the chapel of memories."

"Huh," I say. "Probably not."

"She was older than I thought—sixty-eight. She had grandkids."

"Huh," I say.

"She was awesome. Unlike some people, right? Like anybody would've missed *her* if she was dead."

"Would anyone have missed me?" I ask, and she puts down her bucket and pulls me into a hug. Then she steps back, and I'm surprised to see that her eyes are full of tears. She releases me, picks up her bucket, and continues down the hallway. I turn around, go back inside my tomb, and close the shades.

•

Early April in Howard Hall, a week before Titanic night: white buds on the trees, the days foggy then bright. It was early evening, the clouds dark as bruises. Dr. D had conferences for her English Capstone class, required for students in their last semester of junior year or first semester of senior year, discussing the drafts of their resumes: "Is there anyone besides your aunt Kathy that you could put as a reference?" No one was prepared for the world; good luck finding a job, or love, or keeping your worst impulses at bay, or keeping your shit together, or keeping the ghosts of your past from teaming up with your regrets and punching you awake at three in the morning. Not that she could say any of this out loud.

It was after five o'clock; one more conference to go. She heard the English Department secretary lock up the main office, walk down the hallway talking on the phone, making plans for dinner. In the silence, the weight of loneliness descended. She was overdue for her next sabbatical. She would go somewhere far north this time, where the summer sun never set.

Footsteps: Margaret, whose resume she had given a C-. Margaret, earnest but unoriginal. She sat in the back row and said nothing. But she was only a junior, so there was hope. Under job experience, she had written: *Cafeteria worker, banquet server.* Under references, she had put a question mark. Under skills, she had written: *Pretty fast at typing, can wash dishes.* Under career goals, she had written: *I really just want to make a living and get out of debt.* She'd also handwritten at the top: *Sorry, Dr. D. I guess I don't have much experience with anything!* None of them had much actual experience with anything, but Dr. D liked talking to them. She liked hearing about their older brothers and their sick mothers and their dogs and their vacations to Disney World. She'd suggest they join a club or even better, try study abroad! She liked it when they left her office smiling, hopeful, thinking they weren't such losers. You'll be fine, she liked to tell them, because she usually believed this to be true.

Her phone buzzed with this message: *Campus Alert System. Active shooter reported entering Howard Hall. Shelter in place.*

She rose from her desk, pushed her door shut, and locked it.

The heart, it turned out, was an organ that could expand to fill the entire body: throat, head, knees, lungs, everything had a pulse, even the bones of her fingers.

A knock. "Dr. D?"

It wasn't that she thought Margaret was the shooter, but it wasn't that she didn't think it, either. "Dr. D?" Another knock. But even if she wasn't the shooter, the shooter could be right behind her, could push open the door as soon as Dr. D opened it.

For the first time, Dr. D really paid attention to her office door: a white door, four small panes of frosted glass. A silver handle instead of a knob. Or no, not silver: stainless steel. Next to the door, the pamphlet in every university office and classroom: Emergency Procedures. What to do in case of flood, fire, earthquake. She thought of the online active shooter training, how she was supposed to run, if possible, and if not, then hide. Maybe she should have run.

Her phone lit up again: *Active shooter in Howard Hall. Shelter in place.*

Margaret was a dark shape behind the frosted glass. Dr. D put her face against the door. "Be quiet," she hissed. "Hide." But there was no place to hide, all the offices were locked, and now hers was locked; the restrooms didn't even have locks.

Margaret again: "Please let me in. So I don't fucking die!"

Dr. D's heart pounded out the answer: *No.* Fear was just the will to live, she realized. There was a time not that long ago when she would have been able to fling open the door and risk or even lose her own life to save someone else's, but apparently this was not that time. She sank to the floor. Her body felt heavy as a sarcophagus.

A tall shadow appeared next to Margaret's shadow, and then came Margaret's voice, possibly her last words, hard as revenge: *"There's somebody in there."* The door handle rattled. Dr. D's life didn't flash before her eyes: that was bullshit. Only later would she realize she'd sliced neatly into selves: one forever assessing, *Do you deserve this, whatever it is?* The other forever crouched on the floor, gasping for all the air the world would give her.

•

On Monday, Tara, Curt and Craig burst into the room and Curt pulls off my covers. I'm on the top bunk, so they're below me, staring up. I feel like I'm floating.

"Happy walkout day!" says Tara.

"It's your day, babe," says Curt.

"I'm going to firebomb her house," says Craig.

"What?" I say.

"To avenge you," says Curt.

"Nothing to avenge," I remind him, sitting up and hugging my sweaty pillow.

"Look at you," he says. "You're just a fucking mess."

"They planted a tree for you," says Tara. "And one for Dr. Frame, too." She reaches for my hand and I let her take it. The trees are in the memorial garden by the student union, planted for dead faculty and students. There's some quote by a famous poet on a plaque, but I've never bothered to read it.

Craig pulls open the blinds. The light feels like it's trying to claw its way into my brain, but that's probably because I drank all of Tara's secret stash of root beer schnapps last night. I feel bile rise to my throat. "Get up, stand up," Craig says, like he's Bob Marley. He's wearing a T-shirt with Calvin and Hobbes, and he doesn't look like a firebomber, but I also know that you can never tell what people are capable of.

For instance, I didn't know that I was the type of person who would tell a murderer where an innocent person was hiding. Not that she was all that innocent, and not that he was a murderer: just a clueless seventeen-year-old townie, lost on his way to the music department for a flute lesson. He happened to walk into Howard Hall with what looked like a gun but was actually a flute case as a car backfired and a frightened freshman texted that he'd heard gun shots, and campus police were alerted. When he looked at me—this pasty, brown-eyed stranger—I knew I was dead, and I just wanted her to be dead, too. So I said, "Someone's in there," and gave the door one last try so we could enter together.

"You need to come with us," Curt says, and all I can think to say back is, "I don't love you." He laughs.

So I resurrect myself, still in my raggy sweats, and put on a pair of flip flops and don't bother combing my hair. "You look great," says Tara, by which she means I look awful. She drapes a fleece hoodie over my shoulders, and we all make our way down the empty hallway, down the empty stairwell, the scuffed fake-marble floors, and out the double doors into an afternoon that seems washed clean of all colors but white and pale green. My contact lenses are cloudy with goo. I realize Craig is gone. Tara and Curt are on either side of me. The quad is full of people—students, professors, strangers—shouting and holding signs: *Dr. D Must Go!* and pictures of Dr. Frame with a halo around her gray head, and pictures of me with *Justice for Margaret* scrawled across my neck.

"Isn't this great?" shouts Curt.

"I didn't even study for that history test," shouts Tara.

I feel people touching me, fingers reaching out; somebody puts a crown of daisies on my head and I knock them off and I push my way through, losing Tara and Curt, swan-diving my hands so I can burrow into the body of this crowd, a human-made maze I have to carve through like a worm, tunneling across the grass that was just yesterday full of hacky sackers and a hot air balloon, now gone to who knows where. The crowd thins and I keep running until I reach Howard Hall; no one sees me enter through the side door or take the echoing steps up to the second floor.

The hallway is dim, the offices empty because everyone is outside, shouting about the unfairness of the world. I stop by her door: darkness inside the glass. I think of the last time I was here, the townie and I staring at each other, then campus police storming up the stairs, guns drawn, the boy—his name was Steven Riley—dropping his flute, being tackled to the ground. I heard his parents are suing the college, suing Dr. D, suing the officer who handcuffed him, suing the music teacher who failed to give proper directions.

Dr. D came trembling out of her office, her eyes wide and red. "Margaret," she said. "We were both so frightened."

I turned to the officer holding the handcuffed boy, who was crying. "My professor left me out here to die," I said, and this went in the report, went in the campus newspaper, went online, went everywhere. I waited for Dr. D to say something in her defense, or accuse me of trying to kill her right back, but she didn't. I have the weird thought that she's in there right now. I have the weirder thought that I'm in there, too, that the two of us are sitting in the dark, watching this other me pace outside the door. The panes of glass are cloudy as ice, and I'm just the shadow creature moving toward the surface, then falling away.

Sharon by the Seashore

Sharon sells sex toys by the seashore. She drives her red convertible down the streets of Delray Beach, parks in front of a lemony apartment complex off Ocean Boulevard. The lot is already full of convertibles, many with vanity plates: 2HOT4U, HOTMAMA2, and variations thereof. Inside, the cooing ladies welcome her, their hair frosted and tufted, their bodies shaped like pigeons. Pink tops, white Capri pants, perfect nails, gold rings. Someone pours her a mimosa. The air conditioner hums. The apartment looks like all the other Florida apartments: pale walls with watercolors of seashells and sandy beaches. The morning sun glares through the blinds. She can see the shapes of families headed to the beach with their umbrellas and their towels.

The ladies gather around the glass table where she's set up her wares.

They say: How cute! How adorable! Why, I never saw such a thing! I can't put that up my hoo-ha. Oh ha ha ha!

They buy the vibrators shaped like animals, they buy the fuzzy handcuffs and the nipple clamps and the edible underwear that tastes like fruit rollups. They get drunker and drunker, and one of them begins to cry and the other bird ladies gather around and hug her, and then they hug

Sharon, and then she gathers up her shiny case of treats and gets back in her red convertible.

•

In Sharon's dreams, she is ten years old, knee deep in the surf. A stingray glides past her shins, and she squeals and swims after it. She can still see the red beach umbrella on the shore; she can see her mother in her green dress. Her mother is shouting and waving: *Come back!* But the horizon is a bright fairy calling, and Sharon obeys. The water lifts her up and down, up and down—and then down and over and under. When she surfaces, her mother is running in her long green dress, and the tan boy from the lifeguard tower is running, too. Then the water slams her down again.

In her dreams, she climbs out of the sea to find the tan boy kissing her mother as she lies lovely on the sand. Her mother sits up with a smile. Her hair is crowned with seaweed, and her dress is a net of dancing fishes.

But when Sharon wakes in the heart-pounding night, she knows her mother stayed blue and still. She remembers her father sobbing, and the tan boy falling back on his knees as the ambulance came up the beach, scaring the gulls.

•

Sharon recharges the sex toys in the cigarette lighter as she drives along the seashore. Before she sold sex toys, she sold makeup and essential oils and artisanal soaps and life insurance. The sex toys are a joke and also not a joke. Her last boyfriend said: *What's with all the bells and whistles?* And she said, *Pleasure and pain, baby,* because she knew that was the sort of thing he expected her to say.

But the truth is she likes the sex toys, their dumb colors and obvious shapes and simple purpose. And she likes that the bird ladies gather around her and coo and dance.

They call her adorable and they hug her, and they bring her mimosas and tell her about their daughters who live in Boston or New York City and don't visit enough. They ask about her parents and she tells them her mother is a mermaid and her father lives in a cave, which is pretty much true, seeing as he never leaves his studio apartment in Boca.

They ask about her love life, and she says she knows how to have fun, leaving out the part about nightmares and loneliness and desperately missing her mother.

Now, the sun bouncing off the windshield, she drives down palm-waving streets to a gated community off Atlantic Avenue. She glides past the club house, the swimming pool, the bocce courts, the middle-aged couple walking in their tennis whites, another swimming pool, a green lake with a wooden pier. She parks in front of the four-car garage. The doorbell plays Edelweiss while a lizard darts up the stucco wall. There's the distant sound of a small dog yipping. A gray housekeeper wearing a gray apron opens the door. Her eyes are the color of dust. She gestures wordlessly toward the living room, which Sharon enters with her marvelous case of sex toys.

Young women in very small dresses clap their hands. They're wearing pink paper crowns; there are streamers and champagne glasses and shot glasses. A barefoot young woman wearing a *Bachelorette!* crown shouts, "Ohmygodit'syou!" and barrels across the room, hugs Sharon around the neck. "Guys, everybody," she announces, "we went to *high* school together!"

Now Sharon remembers her. Rose: cheerleader, quizcheater, binge-eater. She'd passed snarky notes in history class. Pushed Sharon into a locker once and tried to pretend it was an accident. She'd stopped talking to her entirely after she found out Sharon's mother was dead: "I just try to think about *good* things," she'd said. And now, ten years later, here she is: skinny and teeter-heeled, drunk, skin cancer tan, grabbing Sharon's elbow and telling her all about her gorgeous fiancé who has a boat.

Sharon nods and smiles as she sets out her devices and gadgets and handcuffs and plastic thingamajigs. The bridesmaids giggle and shove each other, and the gray housekeeper fills their glasses with champagne.

"Why I *never*," says a bridesmaid, and another bridesmaid says, "Well now you *can*."

Sharon does her spiel, her song-and-dance. She pushes the buttons so the bunny vibrators twitch, and the big green dildos swoon like palm trees in a storm. The gray housekeeper offers a tray of crustless sandwiches and when a glass shatters, Rose shrieks: "Clean that up, will you? I'm barefoot!" and the gray housekeeper kneels and sweeps.

"Your mother is cute," says one of the bridesmaids, giggling, and Rose says, "She's a bitch." Sharon remembers now that Rose's father left them senior year, running away with the school librarian. She remembers the gray housekeeper—not a housekeeper at all, but Rose's mother—sitting alone in the back row at graduation.

Rose and her bridesmaids are standing in a circle around the table where Sharon has set out the toys. "Wouldn't he get a kick out of this?" Rose says of the edible underwear. "Is it gluten-free?" she asks Sharon. "Ha ha ha!"

Discussion ensues among the girls about the best ways to conceive while employing the various devices. "Maybe your baby will grow up and sell sex toys," says one of the bridesmaids, and Rose says, "I would kill myself," and they all smile at Sharon, who smiles back.

•

It's not that Sharon condones curses. It's not that she stays up all night plotting ways to exact revenge upon anyone, as if there were anyone to exact revenge upon. Certainly not the tan lifeguard boy who did all he could. Not the man at the Jiffy Lube who charged her double for an air filter, or even her last boyfriend, who broke up with her over an expensive dinner then asked if she would mind paying because he lost his wallet.

After Sharon's mother failed to wake from her watery slumber, Sharon spent a good deal of time in her room with her mother's secret books, the ones hidden in the top cupboard behind the spice rack. From these books, Sharon learned how to teach her cat to shake hands and use a toilet like a human. She made a lizard dance on two legs. She lured a small alligator into the house and taught it to play Crazy Eights. One day, her father opened her bedroom door to find her sitting on the floor playing Monopoly with an alligator, a black bear, and her cat. "Can I play, too?" he asked, but his sadness was too terrible, and she said they were nearly finished, maybe next time.

There were other spells in that book: how to take the firstborn of an enemy is one that currently comes to mind. But what would she do with a baby?

She suspects the black bear is already slinking in from the piney woods behind the bocce courts. The alligator's snout is rising wetly from the green lake. These aren't her childhood friends. She's not sure what they might do.

Rose's mother gives Sharon her credit card and says she'll take everything. When Sharon asks if she's sure, she says, "It's what Rose wants."

Of course she does, Sharon thinks. Of course she wants everything.

"Is that a bear?" someone gasps.

"Is that an alligator?" someone shrieks.

Sharon hopes she's doing this right: the same spell that her mother used to make the fishes dance in her green dress as she died, so that Sharon would not be afraid. But who knows? Let's find out. The bridesmaids step back as the sex toys leap off the table. The dildos hop, the vibrators dance, the handcuffs shimmy, the nipple clamps twirl. The doors to the back yard swing open and here come the bridesmaids, everyone bunny-hopping out onto the lawn as if lured by music only they can hear; and now here comes the black bear, why not, holding out a paw. Bear and bride and bridesmaids and sex toys dancing in a circle.

Love, sex, grief, bears: forces you can tame for a moment, if you're lucky.

A neighbor will capture grainy video footage, but no one will be able to say exactly what it shows, and the bridesmaids will never speak of it.

Rose's mother lets out a gasp of laughter and then she's gone, fleet-footed and shrieking, back through the house and out the front door to the driveway, where the convertible glows in the South Florida sun like something that could blast off. Sharon follows close behind. Rose's mother is already in the passenger seat, buckled up.

"We'll go dancing at Johnnie Brown's," Sharon says, as she climbs behind the wheel. "We'll go to the beach, but not too close to the water. We'll play Monopoly and Crazy Eights."

"Yes," says Rose's mother. She flings her gray apron into the sawgrass, and Sharon backs out of the driveway as an alligator lopes down the lawn with a poodle in its jaws.

Cornfield, Cornfield, Cornfield

Her parents' argument had driven her out of the house, and now she was lost. There was the cornfield, there was the moon. The lights of her neighborhood had vanished. It was past midnight, early August. She would begin eleventh grade next month; summer swimming lessons were over. No more walking with her sister the five blocks to the country club that they were too poor to actually belong to. She was barefoot—big mistake—wearing denim shorts under her nightgown. Her feet hurt, her legs were itchy, and all she could see was cornfield, cornfield, cornfield.

Beyond the cornfields was I-95, heading south to Baltimore, north to Philadelphia, places she would one day live—two years with a rich boyfriend near Harbor Place, six months alone in a studio apartment in Philly, smoking clove cigarettes and drinking Coronas instead of going to her secretarial job, which she would quit when she went back to college, met a man who looked homeless but wasn't, married him, and spent fourteen decent years with him before moving back to her childhood home, where her mother smoked on the sofa until she nearly burned the house down.

Her older self found her younger self in the cornfield and said: *Oh, poor you, a boy you like doesn't like you, and a boy you don't like does like you, and algebra is so hard. Your mother is fat and cries about it; your father is broke and yells about it. Your sister floats sweetly in her own jet stream, with her guinea pigs and her bangles, and she will always be a little happier than you are, and a little more foolish.*

And her younger self didn't pay any attention, because she was thinking that here it was, her last chance to be interesting: vanished, murdered, a mystery, a cult, a tragedy, a warning, forever sixteen years old, a smiling angel in the back of the yearbook. She struggled through the weeds and lifted her young face to the moon—felt the moon staring down and saying, *Oh, you're a remarkable young lady* in the voice of her father for some reason. *Keep on keeping on,* her social studies teacher liked to say, what a nerd, but she kept on keeping on and suddenly there were the lights of her own neighborhood, her own house, her own life welcoming her back.

The house lights were out now; the argument was over. She found the front door unlocked as she'd left it, stepped inside, shut the door behind her. She climbed the carpeted steps to the bathroom she shared with her sister and washed her filthy feet in the bathtub, tenderly, as if they were blind, gentle creatures who loved her.

Rise

The first strange thing was the tooth. Of course, I was used to hearing jokes about putting my heart into my work; blood, sweat and tears, etc. My mother never got tired of telling me that love was the most important ingredient of all, which is, of course, bullshit. But a tooth?

It was the first day I opened the bakery after the funeral—my wife's mother. Seventy-seven years old, brain cancer. We'd gone to Baltimore for the burial and stayed a week. Kathy wasn't taking it well. She crawled into bed the day we got back to Mississippi and didn't get up except to eat a sandwich and use the bathroom. Then the nightmares started bolting her awake every night, shaking. I offered to stay home with her—she's a sixth-grade teacher, off for the summer—but she said no, of course you have to get back to work, I'll be fine.

On the Day of the Tooth—as I later came to think of it—Sherry, the hairdresser from next door, had purchased a loaf of sourdough but came swinging back through the glass doors not ten minutes later.

"Look look look," she said, holding out the remains of the bread on its paper sack.

Teri, who works the counter, drawled, "Well, yuck," and I turned off the mixer and came down to the cash register and peered down at a gold tooth shining in the crumbs.

"Your tooth came out?" I said. This would be bad for business is what I was thinking.

"Not *my* tooth," said Sherry. "I don't have any gold teeth anyway."

"Well, yuck," said Teri again.

"I'm really, really sorry about that," I said. "I have seriously no idea." Could it have been in the flour? That was the only explanation. I took the tooth and the crumbs to the back and returned with a warm baguette. "On the house," I said. "I can personally guarantee there's no teeth in it."

"Hmm," said Sherry and took the baguette with a frown.

"That's just weird is all," said Teri.

"It is pretty weird," I said.

•

A baker's hours are long. As long as you think they're going to be, they're longer. When I opened three years ago—the only artisan bakery in this north Mississippi town—I expected twelve-hour days, but I did not expect ninety-hour weeks. "You're working big-time lawyer hours," Kathy pointed out, "and making a shit salary." I corrected her: "I'm making *no* salary." But I was happy, and she was happy for me. We had no children and had never wanted them. We lived fine—not great, but fine—off of her teaching salary.

Gradually, the bakery began making a small profit: ciabatta buns for wedding receptions, pizza Wednesdays. There were a decent number of regulars, mostly Europeans who taught at the nearby university and missed the bread of their childhood. I hired Teri to work the front counter. I hired a culinary student as an assistant baker, but he didn't catch on; he saw only the technique, not the alchemy. He let the sourdough over-proof a few too many times, so I let him go. I work better alone anyway.

And of course, mistakes happen every day. Sometimes I don't even know why—maybe the air was too humid, or too dry. Maybe I used too much steam, or too little. It's easy for a loaf to sink like a brick, or puff up and collapse. It's *not* so easy for a gold tooth—a molar, from the looks of it—to emerge from an otherwise perfectly baked loaf of sourdough. I considered calling the flour company in North Carolina and complaining.

And then I didn't. I thought: It's a fluke. There's no chance of something like that happening again.

I wanted to tell Kathy about the tooth, but she was asleep when I got home, curled up in a light blanket at the far edge of the bed, her breathing calm and deep. It was August and muggy; the ceiling fan chugged. I felt her forehead: cool, no fever. Strewn across the living room were the contents of the two boxes we'd brought home from her mother's house—photos and toys, some old newspapers. I left them there. I cleaned the cup and plate she'd left in the sink and crawled into bed beside her.

•

The next strange thing was the rabbit. The day after the tooth incident, a twelve-year-old kid came in with his little sister for ciabatta after their karate class like they did every Tuesday, both wearing those white bathrobe-looking outfits. The little girl had a green sash; the boy's was brown. They were always very polite, calling Teri "ma'am." I sometimes stepped out from the back to make a joke about karate-chopping the bread, and this time the boy grinned and pulled it out of its paper sack and kapow, just chopped the thing with his hand. His sister shrieked and clapped. A ciabatta is soft, not exactly breakable, so really he just made a big dent in the middle, but when we'd stopped laughing, we realized that one side of the loaf was moving, and then a gray little paw poked out followed by a gray bunny.

"OMG," said Teri in a way that first made me think she was saying something in a foreign language: *Oemgi.* Japanese for: *small rabbit hops from bread.*

The kids were staring at me like I was a wizard. Teri seemed to be hyperventilating. We watched the bunny's face and ears twitch. It had a cute little white tail. The girl caught it as it was about to hop off the counter.

"Here," I said, grabbing a to-go pizza box. It was just the right size; you could close it and still hear the bunny skittering around in there. "This is for you." I gave them a bunny-free ciabatta, too, squeezing it first to be sure.

"Thanks, mister," the kids intoned, like they were hypnotized, and then backed away and out the door, grinning so hard their little faces looked like they'd break.

"That," I said to Teri when they'd gone, "was not in there when I took it out of the oven."

"*I* didn't do it," she said, defensively. "I need this job."

"I know you didn't," I said. "But maybe we both need to be a little more aware of quality control in the future."

•

That night, the living room was even more of a mess: a couple of her mom's high school yearbooks, some baby pictures of Kathy and her sister. Her parents' wedding photo, both Mom and Dad wearing goofy grins and horn-rimmed glasses. A snow globe of the Grand Canyon, from some trip back in the 1980s. There was no plate in the sink. No cup. Kathy was flat on her back in our bed, arms out to the side, but she was breathing in a peaceful kind of way. "Honey," I said quietly, and nudged her. "Did you eat anything today?"

She mumbled something and pulled the sheet over her head.

"Honey?" I tried again.

"Stop it," she said. "Sleeping."

The next morning, I called Teri and told her to open the shop and sell the day-olds but to close when we ran out; I was taking the day off. At a little after eight, I woke Kathy gently, pulled her from bed, watched her grumpily stomp around and pull on her robe. We sat across from each other at the kitchen table.

"I know this has been hard on you," I said to her. "But you need to take care of yourself. Or let me take care of you."

"I'm fine. I just need to sleep, damn it."

She drank a little of the coffee I put in front of her; then she went out to the living room and sat on the floor in her pajamas with the photos and the toys and the newspaper clippings. I went quietly into the study and worked on the accounts, called Teri to see if anybody had found any more anomalies in the bread. "By anomalies," she said, "do you mean like an eight-track cassette of Earth, Wind and Fire?"

I said yes, that would be an anomaly.

"I'd forgotten all *about* eight-tracks." She sounded delighted. I did not think delighted was the way she should be feeling, so I said, sharply, "What happened? Did someone complain and did you give their money back?"

And she said not exactly, but that Marsha from Regions Bank came in for a day-old whole wheat and when she asked for it sliced, that's when Teri discovered the anomaly. They had a good laugh about disco music and then Teri sliced her up a loaf of day-old rye, even though Marsha made it clear that she had really been hoping for whole wheat.

"Just close up now," I told her. "Just go on home."

I could hear Kathy saying something, so I went out into the living room, and she was pacing, her robe flapping open, shouting into the phone: "But we could have at least had a going away party! We have going away parties for people who fucking retire or move to fucking Florida, but not for this?" I knew she was talking to her sister Roberta even before she said, "She was my mother, too, and I think we should have had a goddamned party." Then she flung the phone across the room, where it bounced off the television set with a thwack. When she looked at me, her eyes were red-rimmed and furious. "I'm awake. Are you happy?"

I told her I wasn't.

"Go feed your damn mother," she said.

•

When customers ask me for my "recipe," I play along. "Flour," I say, ticking off on my fingers. "Salt. Water." Sometimes they get annoyed with me: No, really, don't be coy, and I say I'm not being coy, that's what bread *is*. But it's also timing. Think of a party, I might say if anyone cared to hear me explain it. You can arrive too early, when no one is mingling or dancing yet. You can arrive too late, when the food is gone and everyone's drunk and tired. What you want to do is arrive at the perfect moment so you can have a great time. For bread, the perfect moment is when you've fed your mother starter and the dough begins to rise and bubble. When the dough doubles in size, you shape the loaves. When those double, you bake. Mess up the timing, and you arrive at the party when everyone's looking for their keys, saying goodbye.

I have filled trash bins of loaves that were hard and flat as baseball mitts. Sometimes I never know what I did wrong, or why the bread wanted more than I could give it. So when Kathy told me to go take care of things at the bakery, I went; and when I came home an hour later she was asleep, as I knew she would be, curled up on the living room floor, mouth open, eyes fluttering behind her lids as she dreamed and dreamed.

•

The next morning, the dough looked good. It *felt* good. It folded and rose as it should; it baked up brown and lovely.

I poked a knife into every loaf, carefully. And so I was not only perplexed but frustrated—infuriated, really—when Teri called out, "What the?" as she was slicing the rye for the ham and cheese lunch special.

She was holding up a noisemaker. She put it to her lips and blew and the curly cootie-tongue flew out and screeched. "This could be fun," she said, because she saw the look on my face. "People might buy these on purpose?"

I grabbed the rye and swooped the rest of the bread off the shelves onto the floor while she leapt back. "Go home," I told her, and she said, "You're just having a bad week," as she pulled off her apron. When she'd gone, I flipped the Open sign to Closed and set about slicing every loaf I'd already baked: the Kalamata olive, the rosemary raisin, the baguettes. It was a waste, a horrible waste, surely there couldn't be anything else, could there? Was I really such a terrible baker that pretty much anything at all could end up in my loaves?

And then I pulled on a foil scroll rolled up in a rosemary raisin, and a banner unfurled: *Bon Voyage!* it said in sparkly purple. And another, in gold: *Good luck on your new adventure!*

And one more, in solemn black and white, rolled up in a loaf of rye: *We will miss you.*

•

It's not exactly true that Kathy's mother died of brain cancer. She had brain cancer, yes, and it certainly would have killed her, which she was well aware of. She'd had headaches. She'd fainted in the nut aisle at Safeway, knocking out a tooth. There were tests. And then she sent an email to Kathy, Roberta, and their father, her ex-husband:

Hey guys, no point putting us through all that crap again (you know what crap). I'm going to take care of things on Tuesday. The house deed is in the credenza.

Love, Mom (Judy)

Kathy called right away, of course, and her mother said, "A bottle of pills. Some vodka. Easy breezy."

"But, Tuesday?" said Kathy. It was Sunday. "That's so soon."

And then her mother said on second thought, it was a beautiful day and she was feeling great, why wait for another headache?

I told Kathy I'd be the one to call 911, and she said, "But it's what Mom wants. Roberta and Dad agree." They'd all been through this long before I met Kathy, with her grandmother. A long, terrible death. That night, Kathy and I went out with some friends and drank a lot of martinis, and I was so drunk I don't remember getting home. The next morning, we were woken by Roberta calling from Baltimore to tell us Judy was gone.

•

"Your dreams are turning up in my bread," I said to Kathy that night. She was snoring quietly on the living room sofa. "This is why you aren't waking up from nightmares anymore."

She snored on.

I sat on the floor and sorted through the photos and the clippings and toys. Kathy and Roberta and their mother with a little gray rabbit. (*Fletcher,* someone had written in pencil on the back.) Judy at the Baltimore zoo, hugging herself in front of a boa constrictor cage. Photos of Kathy's young parents on a dance floor under a disco ball. The whole family wearing Mickey Mouse ears. There was an ancient Barbie wearing a pea-green dress that smelled vaguely of vomit.

Until Kathy had dreamed her way through this, there was no telling what might turn up in my loaves. Boa constrictors? Mouse ears? I called Teri and told her I was closing the shop for the near future. I told her I understood if she needed to look for another job.

She wasn't happy. "Is it the anomalies?" she asked, and I said it was.

•

At first, I was curious, and I cut each loaf carefully open: a summer sandal, a hermit crab, a Christmas ornament. But soon I realized there was no time for this. Some of the loaves were moving; some seemed to be singing. I heard the ocean in one, a roller coaster in another. I ran the oven night and day, losing track of all time except the time that mattered: bread time. The proofing, the rising, the baking.

It was, I admit, my best work. I'd never baked such perfectly crispy sourdoughs, such gorgeous ryes, or ciabatta that seemed light enough to float—and one of them actually did float. I ran out of space in the front room so I got a step ladder and stacked the loaves to the ceiling, then piled them up against the back wall and on top of the mixer, leaving only a tiny path to the proofing table and the oven.

And finally, there was no room for that anymore. I took out the last batch of twenty-four sourdough and stacked them all around me and above me, until all I could see was darkness, and all I could touch on all sides was bread, and I knew—at last—that Kathy was dreaming of me.

Hematite, Apatite

The principal leaned across his desk at Jennifer and cleared his throat. He was a small man with small hands, and these hands, she noticed now, were trembling. "It has come to my attention," he said, "that there have been accusations."

"Oh, no," said Jennifer. Her head ached. She'd had too much cheap Australian Chardonnay last night and called her third ex-husband in Newark, waking his wife. This was, she knew, shameful behavior for a woman of nearly sixty— or for any age at all, really. Maybe the students had noticed a lingering odor of wine and tears, or a general sense of malaise, or maybe someone had reported that she'd said "Damn" last week when she slammed her finger in her desk. And she'd called that Simpson girl a silly fool—but that was a joke. The girl had laughed. Hadn't she?

"Of witchcraft, you see," the principal said. He seemed a little apologetic. "The Darnell twins say they saw you flying through the forest above Wheel Road on their way home from ballet class last night."

"But I was at home." This could be confirmed. Her ex-husband's current wife would remember; and there was evidence in the trashcan: that empty bottle of penguin wine. She felt herself begin to relax.

The principal, however, did not seem relaxed; he was clenching his teeth in what was probably supposed to be a smile. "Of course, their mother didn't see a thing. But she was driving, you see. Eyes on the road." His hands were clasped on his desk like the children were instructed to do for school portraits.

Jennifer nodded. Her mouth felt dry.

"You will have a chance to defend yourself. But for now." He unclasped his hands, shrugged. In the five years he'd been principal of the middle school, he had lost his wife to cancer and his parents in a drunk driving accident. He had given eulogies for two seventh graders who slit their wrists in a suicide pact. He was, like the principal before him, a transplant from a northern city who came to Mississippi either out of optimism or desperation. There had been speculation that he was about to take early retirement and move back to the north. There were rumors of a daughter in jail. And now here was yet another burden thrust upon him. Jennifer felt a twinge of pity for the man. She said, "I'm sure we can sort this out easily enough. Sixth graders are pretty imaginative."

The principal nodded. "I'm afraid we have to put you on leave, you see. For the rest of the day, and until we get this sorted out. We have a sub coming in after lunch. The hearing is set for tomorrow at two-thirty in the conference room." He cleared his throat, scooted back in his chair, and waited for Jennifer to stand; then he thrust out a small, moist, trembling hand for her to shake.

"Please tell the sub that the lesson plan is in the blue binder," Jennifer said. "We're covering igneous and sedimentary this week." She thought of the box of rock samples she'd set out last night, drunkenly, on her dining room table: their rough surfaces, their ancient mysteries. She was not going to hand those over to the sub.

"Will do," said the principal. "Don't you worry."

•

Ex-husband number four, Richie, was in the back of his restaurant marrying ketchups when she came in through the side door. She had met him during her brief stint as a waitress at the Pig Palace, an upscale barbeque restaurant popular with the graduation and prom crowd. Then, he was a jokey manager; now, he was the owner and was pretty much always in a bad mood. His beard was turning into one of those mountain-man-type things, and his belly hung low over his khaki pants, but there was still something appealing about him when he smiled. Their marriage had been marked by anger and betrayal on both sides, but that was almost a decade ago—which was long enough for bygones to be bygones. She hoped.

"You heard any rumors about me?" she asked abruptly when he looked up from the ketchups.

"You mean did I spread any rumors about you," he said. One of the things she had most loved and most hated about him was his ability to know exactly what she meant whether she said it or not. He looked up, wiped his hand across his nose. "I don't care what you do, sweetheart, as long as you save some sugar for me." This was a song he'd written for her when they'd first dated. "But my mother heard you were out at Chili's until closing on Friday with some motorcycle dude."

"Oh," she said, and blushed. Jake. He didn't have a motorcycle, but he was bald and had tattoos and wore shiny black boots, so of course Richie's mother—who had spies everywhere, apparently—would jump to this conclusion. "That was nobody," she said.

Richie frowned as if he didn't believe her, then shrugged. "Why ain't you at school anyway?" She ignored him. He gave the last ketchup one joyous, farty squeeze, then sneezed into his arm crack.

"God bless you," she said, more sincerely than usual.

•

Her best friend Carlene, who taught history at the high school, said, "Oh, right, like in Norway." Jennifer could hear her munching on something on the other end of the line. Or what was it called now? Not a line. There used to be a line when she was a child—a black phone with a curly-tail cord and a line that traveled for thousands of miles under the earth and the sea.

Yes: Norway rang a distant bell. There was something going on in Norway with witches. Jennifer was bad at keeping up with international news, or any news at all. It probably wouldn't help matters that she was Norwegian, distantly, and that she'd gone back to her very-Norwegian-sounding maiden name.

"What are they doing in Norway?" she asked.

"Covens, devil proms, bewitched pets, that sort of thing. Husbands wander off in the night and come back covered in soot. Women flying on brooms. Just, you know, a lot of weird shit, and so they've started burning them. Hold on a sec, need a swig of water."

Jennifer waited. There was nothing like silence in a lonely house to make you realize how lonely you were. She could hear the squirrels in gutters begin their nightly scuffling. She could hear her stomach rumble; she was on her third diet of the year, this one based entirely on fruits and saltines. Wine, she figured, was allowed, because it was fruit. When Carlene came back, Jennifer ventured to ask, "They've started burning what, exactly?" and Carlene said, "Witches," and Jennifer sighed and said, "I thought so."

"I wouldn't worry too much about it," Carlene said. "They'll do a background check, and you'll come out all right."

"Oh, I know. I'm silly to worry. But it's Box of Rocks week, and I was looking forward to it." Technically, it was called the Earth Science Unit. After all that studying of atomic particles, she was always happy to teach something solid, something that felt real. After Earth Science, they'd get to worm dissection, her least favorite of the units. "We still on for wine night tomorrow?" They met every Wednesday at a café on Main Street to drink wine and complain about their students.

"Well, I don't know," said Carlene. "I think I have papers to grade."

•

October in Mississippi was humid, the leaves turning golden but clinging to the branches, the grass somehow both parched and moist. College students were still biking down Main Street in their shorts and T-shirts. Her bird feeder was full of fat cardinals and squabbling titmice. She had arrived in Mississippi over thirty years ago with ex-husband number one, who debarked for Minnesota after two years. It still felt like a strange, foreign place—or maybe she just felt like a strange foreigner in it. There were moments when she still couldn't understand what people were saying, like when she got a flu shot and the nurse kept asking her if she had a favor and Jennifer said, "You want me to do you a favor? I have no idea what you're talking about," and the nurse said, in a sharp, nasty voice, "A *fever.*" Then plunged the needle into Jennifer's arm with a little too much force.

She drove to the middle school with her windows open, the car full of hot, swampy air. Had they already done a background check on her? To make sure she wasn't talking to anybody in Norway? But that might not be enough. Maybe they would—or had already—talked to her neighbors, who would no doubt call her aloof, rude. She never answered the door when she saw a kid standing on the porch with a box of candy to sell, or a woman with a clipboard. And had she posted anything stupid on her Twitter account? Had she liked anything on Facebook that she shouldn't have liked, or not liked something she should have?

The principal was already in the conference room when she arrived at exactly two-thirty, as were the Darnell twins, looking bored, and their wide-cheeked mother, and a woman in a blue pantsuit who introduced herself as the school district's lawyer. The lawyer put her phone in the middle of the table and said, "I'm recording this, if you don't mind."

"And what if I do?" Jennifer said, trying for a joke, but it didn't come out that way, and the proceedings deteriorated from there. The principal took notes in a black spiral notebook as the Darnell twins recounted seeing Jennifer on a broom above them at eight forty-five on Monday night.

"Because ballet lets out at eight-thirty," said Lorraine, the smallest and most talkative twin. "And then we change our shoes and go outside to wait for Mommy." She had a long, narrow face, her features too close together, her teeth too big for her mouth. Jennifer felt a sudden pang of sympathy for her, always in the shadow of her round-faced sister, Marie, who now smiled sweetly and announced, "I tried to film her but then whoosh, she disappeared."

In Jennifer's classroom, the twins sat next to each other in the front row and only rarely had to be separated for giggling. Last week, they had each made hundred percents on the parts of the Earth quiz. Marie had misspelled *mantle,* but Jennifer gave her full credit anyway.

"Even if I *could* fly through the forest," Jennifer said, trying unsuccessfully to make eye contact with the twins, "why would that automatically make me a bad person?"

The twins' mother perked up. "Why not use your car? If you have nothing to hide?"

"But where would I be *going?*" Jennifer asked, and she realized she actually wanted to know. She'd passed out on the sofa on Monday evening, and so maybe—not that she could recall—maybe she *had* flown on a broom through the forest. Wouldn't that be more interesting than passing out on the couch?

"Devil's mass," said the principal. "Blood sacrifices. Of animals and infants, you see."

"Everyone knows witches eat children," said Marie, a little haughtily.

"That's not something I would do, Marie," Jennifer said. "Plus, I'm on a diet!" Nobody laughed. Her stomach rumbled as if testifying on her behalf. "Anyway," she continued, trying to sound more teacher-like, "the idea of me flying through the air is nonsense. The nature of matter refutes this possibility, and what about the wind resistance required just to keep the broom aloft?"

"And yet we are all made of atoms, are we not?" the principal said with a tight smile. His brow was sweating. "Energy travels in waves, does it not?"

"The children recorded their observations," the twins' mother said, prompting her daughters to pull out their backpacks and rummage through the contents to extract their field notebooks, the ones Jennifer had distributed to the students last week. They had drawn graphs with each inch equaling four feet. "They estimate your flying height at forty-five feet and your speed at fifty miles per hour based on the fact that I was driving thirty-five."

Jennifer frowned. It was somewhat impressive. She pointed to a black line in the center of Marie's page. "That's supposed to be me?"

"That's you," piped up Lorraine. Her graph was sloppier than her sister's; she seemed a little ashamed.

"Do you have *pets?*" the lawyer demanded, pointing at Jennifer with her pen. "Do you have *children?*"

"I had a cat once," Jennifer said. She'd had an abortion between husbands number one and two, but she didn't mention this. "It lived to be twenty-four. It was practically a world record."

The lawyer seemed dismayed by this. "Please enter!" she shouted, and a sheepish, stocky bald man pushed open the conference room door and stood there staring. "Hey," he said to Jennifer. Jake: they'd met when he repaired her brake pads. She'd called him Jake Brake. They'd been on two dates, two! He was fifty-five, with an ex-wife in Wisconsin and two grown sons. They hadn't even slept together. So why was he now standing at the head of the table and telling everyone that she seemed a little pushy, a little desperate, that she had eaten half of the nachos he'd ordered, that she'd had two glasses of wine to his one beer? That she'd told him some of her students were idiots? "I never did," she lied, but then Richie was suddenly ushered into the room as well and stood next to Jake. They didn't look at each other. They didn't look at her. Richie's face was red, and his nose was chapped. He turned to the lawyer. "She gave me a cold," he said, and sneezed. "With her witchcraft."

The lawyer dismissed them. The conference room door wheezed shut. The twins appeared to be texting under the table. "We have other witnesses," the lawyer said, and Jennifer said, "I imagine you do."

Ex-husband number one: what would he say about her? That she'd had a temper, smoked some weed. Ex-husband number two had died of cancer in his mid-forties, three years after they'd divorced because of *his* temper. Then there was ex-husband number three, who'd moved to Newark and sent her a Christmas card every year but never seemed to want to talk on the phone. Maybe she had become increasingly difficult as she got older. Maybe she wasn't fun-loving Jenny anymore. More and more, everything ached—her knees, her neck—and she tended to cuss loudly when she drove. She had not visited her parents' graves in years. She was not a terrible person, but she was not a good person, either. This had not particularly bothered her until now.

"We would hate to bring in the police," the principal was saying, "but it may be necessary. There are tests, you see, that involve ice water and needles and things like that. You should understand how that goes—testing hypotheses and such." He smiled, then sighed. "It's going to be a lot of work for everybody."

Jennifer felt weak with hunger and fury. She had been in this room for over three hours. Her stomach seemed to be eating itself. "If I confess, will that make it easier? Fine, I'm a witch. You're going to fire me anyway. Don't dunk me in ice water to see if I float or not. I've had swimming lessons since I was five."

The lawyer made a quick note.

"Can we go?" said Marie Darnell. "We have flute."

The lawyer clicked off her recording. She nodded at Jennifer. "We'll be in touch if we need anything else."

•

When she was a child in Maryland, Jennifer had irritated her father with her backyard excavations: a bone! An arrowhead! A fossil! A shard of pottery from an ancient civilization! She would burst panting and filthy into the living room, where her father was watching Lawrence Welk. No, Jenny, put that back; stop it, Jenny, that's where we buried Flowers, remember? That's just a rock. That's just a piece of plastic.

But she knew what she knew. The earth was full of secrets. The rock was not just a rock. Her mother was a fossil preserved in amber, a memory of green polyester, pink toenails, paperclip necklaces made by her students. A snowy car crash just yards from the house. Her father's choking sobs. The day after her mother's death, the world was a sheet of ice, and now some of that ice had turned into stones and twinkled in the yard and the driveway.

Well, why not? she thought later, turning over a piece of quartzite in high school geology. The truth was just as unfathomable as anything else. Later, in college, she endured student teaching, she wore her mother's paperclip necklaces. She didn't like children, but she didn't hate them, and sometimes their eyes would actually light up like they were supposed to. Mostly, their eyes stayed dim—in Maryland, in Mississippi, everyone had their own problems, and parents always had something to complain about: Billy didn't have time to study for his test, Kelly's lab partner scared her, Lily had a moral objection to dissecting frogs.

But everybody loved Box of Rocks week. Actually, it was two boxes—one containing rocks, the other minerals—both made of sturdy oak; their lids locked with tiny gold latches. There were twelve specimens in each box, nestled in their own felt-lined compartments. Sometimes she told the students that she had collected them all herself, rock hunting with her father when she was a child, but this was a lie. Her father didn't take her rock hunting. She'd found a slick piece of fool's gold once, hiking in Pennsylvania with husband number one, but she'd tossed it into the trees.

This year, she had decided, she would take the children to the Petrified Forest near Flora. The principal had given his blessing; the parental consent forms were stacked on her desk, ready to distribute. But now the town was full of witches, and no one cared about fossils. She followed the news on her iPad with a mixture of relief and concern. The week after she confessed, four other women were accused: the woman who worked the night shift at the B-Quick, a Mennonite woman who sold banana bread at the farmer's market, a high school English teacher, a Walmart employee. All denied the accusations, some more loudly than others.

At the police station, a make-shift ice pond was constructed. The Walmart employee drowned and was exonerated, but the others were thrown into jail. Their accusers—middle school and high school girls—gave giddy interviews to the local media, lifting up their tops to reveal bruises where the witches had pinched them in the middle of the night. One girl fell to the ground in convulsions when the female news reporter asked her if she was aware of the seriousness of the charges. The news reporter was jailed the next day.

Jennifer ventured rarely from the house. Sometimes she went to Kroger at three in the morning, when the only

customers were other wide-eyed, nervous women, filling
their carts with beer and vegetables and microwavable dinners. She spent her days watching television and reading
mystery novels and, at night, digging through her yard
for more rock samples: granite, shale, a sliver of petrified
wood. A gray rabbit slipped into her tomato garden, and
she trapped it with an Amazon box and then, to her own
surprise, skinned it and roasted it over her fire pit. So much
for her fruit and cracker diet. She felt her muscles growing
strong and taut; under a waxing moon, she leapt up to a
magnolia branch and managed two pullups before collaps-
ing to the ground.

•

And the girls began to roam the streets in small groups,
singing pop songs, stealing clothes from local shops and
falling into occasional convulsions. They accused the mothers of the boys they liked; when the boys agreed to go out
with them, the convulsions stopped. When the boys broke
up with them, the girls twisted and shrieked and said
they could see the boys' mothers flying through the air all
around them, pinching and biting. They accused their own
mothers, who kicked and cursed as they were tossed into
the back of police cars. Jennifer watched the YouTube videos the girls posted, their eyes rolled back to the whites as
they danced and flailed outside the houses of their teachers
and former babysitters.

But no one came to Jennifer's house. Even on Halloween, as the girls roamed the streets, breaking windows
and stealing cash and electronics from abandoned homes,
they left her alone. The town had emptied of adults and
boys, who escaped with their wives and mothers to the
north, or to Alabama or Louisiana. Jennifer stayed in her
house, watched from the curtains. A tiny girl stood in the
moonlight, crying for her mother, and an older girl grabbed
her hand and pulled her roughly down the pavement.

At night, in dreams, Jennifer soared over houses and fields, the cotton fat and white against the thick gray sky. There was no broom, just her body flat against the wind, the air blowing through her teeth.

•

The B-Quick cashier was the first to burn. Her granddaughters said she'd escaped her cell and flown around their bedrooms, spitting and biting. They said she tried to make them do their homework on a Saturday and chewed all their pencils to nubs.

Then Jennifer's friend Carlene burned, shaking her fists at the sky and vowing to return as a haunting spirit. Jennifer watched this all on her iPad, videos filmed and uploaded by the accusing girls, who had started their own YouTube channel. She laughed out loud when she saw the footage of Richie's ninety-year-old mother being hauled down the pavement toward the courthouse. The police and the lawyers had left town, so the older girls served as cop, judge, jury, jailer; they drew straws to see who would get to light the match and toss it onto the pyre.

On Thanksgiving morning, as Jennifer chewed on the leftovers of a rabbit carcass at her dining room table, the doorbell rang. Outside, a shivering woman she almost recognized: oh, yes, the twins' mother. She was gaunt, her eyes opals. "I'm a witch, too," she said when Jennifer opened the door. "Nobody believes me. My children think I'm faking. My husband left town with the algebra teacher." She gazed hopefully into Jennifer's house, hugging herself for warmth. "I was just hoping you would accuse me publicly, since no one else will."

"No," said Jennifer, and she closed the door. The twins' mother stayed on the porch for another couple of hours, then disappeared down the street.

November slipped into watery-skied December. The town was nearly deserted; no one remained but girls with their loud laughter and their dancing. The grocery shelves were empty of food, the library and all the books had burned. Jennifer read and re-read her field guides, did her students' quizzes and worksheets, ate weeds and squirrels and rabbits and roots.

Her third ex-husband's current wife called to say she was worried. Shouldn't Jennifer get out of that crazy town? Come to Newark, she said. They had witches, too, but the cops just gave them fines—twenty bucks, maybe forty. At the most, it was a misdemeanor. "You can't teach school here, of course," she said, "but I can help you find a job as a cleaning woman or maybe a gardener or a night shift convenience clerk."

Then her ex-husband got on the phone and said they were serious, come stay with them. Jennifer tried not to laugh. The yard was full of animal bones. Move to New Jersey and get a job as a night shift convenience clerk? She said, "I will figure something out."

•

Amazing, wasn't it, how desire—for talk, for nourishment—could become a solid artifact? She dreamt not just of flying now, but of her own sixth grade self, alone in the yard, the driveway, hunting for something to make her father look up from his television program and love her again. But she was also herself, and all her other selves, the self with husband numbers one through four, and this new self, strong and hardened, all her layers cemented together. At some point, she realized, her sixtieth birthday had come and gone. In the mirror, her face was all angles and a shock of white eyes and hair and teeth.

She devoured the wilted dandelion weeds. Winter wheat. Sometimes she heard children's laughter or sobs in the distance and thought of all the things she hadn't had a chance to teach this year—not just rocks, but the parts of a worm, the frog. We are animals, we are atoms. Hunger and loneliness: who could tell the difference? On a crisp, moon-filled December evening, she went out the front door for the first time in weeks, ventured all the way to the street carrying her box of minerals: quartz, mica, talc, barite, flu-orite, calcite, pyrite, gypsum, feldspar, olivine, hematite, apatite. A trail right up to her front door—to catch the sun-light and the moonlight. There were so many motherless children crying out for knowledge. All they had to do was look down, follow the glinting path, and she would bring them inside, let them see the Box of Rocks; she would lead them out the back door to the fire pit, offer them food and warmth.

Of course you can hold them, she would say, clicking open the gold latch of the wooden box: this is sandstone, granite, basalt. She thought of the black lump of iron heavy in their palms. Then she would urge them close to the fire, and closer still, until they could feel what it was like to be right inside the Earth's molten heart.

Fillies

At the bar, I pretend to be blind, and Sheila pretends to be deaf. It's a thing we're trying, to avoid what happened last time. Sheila has a deaf dad, so she's fluent in sign language, and I'm good at staring straight ahead. Because I'm pretending to be blind, my other senses are heightened. I can tell that the bartender uses the same body spray as my ex-boyfriend — pinecone scented, even though my ex-boyfriend never went near a pinecone. I can feel every sharp rip in the vinyl bar stool — which is red, even though I'm not supposed to know that. There's a chalkboard advertising two-for-one Jäger shots and a stuffed deer head on the wall, its antlers strung with fairy lights, but I keep staring straight ahead.

The bar is next to a Dollar Store and across the street from a B-Quick, five miles from the university where I'm flunking out of a major I haven't even declared yet. Sheila and I grew up together in Jackson, and our parents thought if we went to State together, we'd keep each other in line. Mostly, this hasn't happened. Mostly, since we have excellent fake IDs, we go to bars and men ask us if we're sisters. Sometimes we say we are; we say our names are Candy and Mandy, and when the men make disgusting suggestions, we laugh and say, "Oh, you wish." Then they call us bitches. When we tell the truth—"No, we're not sisters!"—we get even more disgusting suggestions. They call us worse things than bitches.

According to my actual sister, these things wouldn't happen if we just didn't go to bars. She's thirty years old and lives in Tuscaloosa, married to a youth pastor who is too old for her. They met when she was a youth and he was *much* too old for her, and now they have four children. I tell her that if she'd gone to more bars, maybe she wouldn't have so many children, and she just says, "I'll pray for you."

The bartender looks like a college guy, like any guy from any back row of any of the classes I've flunked. He's got a goatee and he's wearing a Def Leppard T-shirt and I want to ask him why, but because I'm supposed to be blind, I stare past his ear and say, "Hi, there, can we get a couple of Bud Lights?" and he says, "Yep," and doesn't seem to notice anything weird.

Sheila smiles at me like she's thinking maybe this won't be so bad. Maybe this won't be like what happened last time. Not that I'm supposed to be able to see her smiling. She spells something into my hand, à la Anne Sullivan, and I pretend to understand what she's saying.

"She said she's paying," I say to the bartender who is finally like, "Oh, hey, you're blind," and I'm like, "Yeah, and she's deaf," and he's like, "That's cool," and I think, hey, this experiment is going pretty well so far. Sheila slaps down some cash, and the bartender gives her a thumbs-up.

It's Thursday Happy Hour, late in spring semester, and the place is already filling up with groups of frat boys and sorority girls, and some middle-aged professors, and in the back there's a family having a birthday party with two little girls. You'd think that in a bar that has birthday parties for little kids, you wouldn't have to fend off drunken assholes, but you would be wrong. Sheila and I came here once last year, and a dude who had to be at least as old as my sister's husband planted himself at our table and started telling us how pretty we were. We know we're pretty; we don't need some snaggle-toothed guy to tell us that. But we laughed and said thank you, but no thank you, etc. and he stood up and said, "Fine, you think you're too good for me, fine." And we felt bad.

For a while, we only went to bars in a group, which meant me plus Sheila plus whatever guy we trusted, like my boyfriend, or when he turned out to be screwing a girl from his bio class, our friend Rob, who is very big and also very gay, and therefore perfect. One's always enough. When we went in a group, no one bothered us, but we still couldn't have the kind of conversations we needed to have. Like I couldn't complain about my boyfriend when he was sitting right there. And Sheila couldn't tell me about the nightmares starring her mother's boyfriend, which were very specific and maybe have something to do with what actually happened. It's easier to talk about those things in a bar, with some draft beer. It's easier than when we're just sitting around our apartment, where our microwave is busted and the carpet stinks of the last tenant's cat and everything feels kind of doomed.

A dude in a tan visor shoves up next to me. His frat brothers are squeezing in behind him, and because I'm blind I can feel them up behind me, staring down my shirt. One of the dudes rests his elbow on my shoulder like I'm a piece of furniture. "Hey," I say, turning around and staring past him, like I have some idea of where he is but not exactly. Sheila launches into a flurry of sign language, and the dudes are like, "Whoa," and back off.

So Sheila and I *can* have a beer at a bar and not get hit on. The problem, of course, is that we can't really have a conversation with each other. But we're having a pretty good time anyway, and we clink beer bottles and even though I'm not supposed to be able to see her, I do, and she looks relieved. Like what happened last time is not going to happen.

We don't talk about what happened last time. I'd just broken up with my ex, and Sheila had just slept with someone who was texting her constantly and calling her a slut, and we were like, "Let's get out of our shitty apartment and have a goddamn drink." We went to a bar in the next town where we wouldn't run into anyone we know, one of those bars that has bags of pork rinds hanging from the wall, one of those bars where you can still smoke, because no one gives a shit. Yes, we were dressed up, in our rompers and our strappy heels. Yes, we were the only women in the place, which was tiny, just a bar and two little tables and some draft Pabst, and at first, we thought, *Should we?* Then we figured, what the hell.

There were two of them. We let them buy us beers because it seemed easier. We let them tell us how pretty we were, and we said thank you, because we weren't raised to be rude. We laughed when they asked if we were sisters. Then we said stop it. We said really, we mean it, stop it. We left, and they followed us, and one of them grabbed Sheila by the hair, and when we finally got in our car and locked the door and drove off, they followed us for a few miles, really close, like they meant business.

But now. I can smell these dudes before I see them, sweat and cheese fries and stale beer. There are two of them, because there's usually two of them. Sometimes they're young. These ones are old. Backward baseball caps. Khaki shorts and beer bellies. The one next to me says, "Hey," and the one next to Sheila says, "You're a couple of pretty little fillies."

This is a new one. Fillies. I wonder if he might have a little daughter at home who plays with those plastic horses. I used to have the whole set, but Misty of Chincoteague was my favorite. I would gallop her around the kitchen until my mother yelled at me to get out of the way.

"I'm blind," I say, because they don't seem to get that. "And she's deaf. But she can read lips."

This, I realize, was the wrong thing to say, even though it seemed like a good line in our apartment.

"Can she read my lips?" the one next to Sheila asks, leaning closer. She ducks away.

"Please leave us alone," I say, staring at the other guy's ear, which is ugly. "I'm blind, and I'm just trying to have a beer with my deaf friend here."

I'm hoping the bartender will jump in and say, "Hey, buzz off," because creeps sometimes listen to bartenders. But the bartender is hanging out at the other end of the bar, laughing with a couple of girls who look more underage than we are.

What we're supposed to do, so we don't get attacked and then followed home: laugh, laugh and smile, say thank you, say sure, why not, that's so nice of you, thank you, thank you, and then go home with them voluntarily and get naked and do whatever they want. Another option is to cry, or back away, scared, while they grin and say, "You think you're too good for us?"

Instead, I rise from my chair with a great whinny. I paw at the ground with my feet. Sheila jumps up and does it, too. The men are like: *the fuck*? We gallop around the tables of frat boys and sorority girls and middle-aged professors, whinnying and tossing our hair. We gallop around the table with the birthday party, and the little girls say, "Horsie!" and reach toward us.

I will feel bad and stupid about this later, and Sheila and I will never go drinking at this bar again, and actually we won't go to any bar again together, ever. We gallop out the door and into the parking lot, where it's still daylight and the air feels hot and mean in my lungs. We gallop down the sidewalk, our heels clomping, our hands crooked into hooves, past the B-Quick and the Dollar Store. After a few blocks we stop, winded.

We look at each other like we wish we could laugh, but we can't. Instead we turn and walk like our normal selves back up the sidewalk, back to the parking lot, where the birthday party family is standing in front of their SUV. The mother sees us and pushes her daughters into the car. She slides the door shut, like she can stop them from turning into girls like us.

Basic Commands

When I am ten and my sister Mel is seven, we roam the woods behind our house because we are explorers; we are Bigfoot hunters; our heels are shiny-hard and bumblebees tremble in our wake. On Saturdays we climb the fence where our fat cat Patches keeps lazy watch, and we pick our way through the poison oak and the wild garlic, all the way to the dirt road that leads to Maureen Ray's house, where—in the front yard—her stepfather pulls the heads off snapping turtles to make soup. Maureen is in my grade; in four years she will drop out of school, pregnant, and my mother will say, "Her mother should have kept an eye on her, seeing as how slow she is," and I will think, Oh, right, she's *slow,* and forgive myself just a little for being mean to her, and then immediately feel worse about being mean to her.

Mel and I are headed for the cold stream behind Maureen's house; sometimes we hear yelling or a loud TV coming from up the hill where Maureen lives with her older sister and her mother and stepfather and her Weebles Treehouse, which I covet. We know, because our favorite show is *In Search Of,* that Bigfoot is reclusive and that his footprints are often hard to distinguish, but we distinguish them in the red clay and we follow them out to the gravel road that leads back to our house. We make it home before the sun goes down, and our mother is sitting in the kitchen talking on the phone; the light falls across the table and makes her look warm and tired, which she is; and our father is tucked away downstairs in his study clattering away on his typewriter—working on his novel about an iceberg that destroys New York City.

Years later, my sister and I will marvel at our parents' ignorance at letting us wander off for entire days—that it was the 1970s seems like no excuse. It's a miracle we weren't kidnapped, we say, or hacked to death by Maureen's crazy stepfather, or turned into druggies by Maureen's glamorous disco-dancing sister.

My sister's pets are all microchipped, and I can go for days without leaving my house. Sometimes weeks.

●

Twenty-six years after our Bigfoot-hunting summer, my sister agrees to let me stay in her guestroom for a week. "Two at the most," I say, and she says, "That's cool." She and her husband, George, live in a big pink house in Roanoke, Virginia with their ten-year-old daughter, Amber. When you walk into the house, your eyes and throat burn. Three dogs bark psychotically from the basement, and five cats poke their heads over the railing, and from down the hall, there's a frantic squawking from the parakeet. Only the angelfish are silent and scentless, swimming round-eyed in their big tank in the living room.

Mel takes me downstairs to the basement, shouting, "Down! Down!" at the three dogs. Two are solid, anvil-headed females, and one is a wriggling male beagle puppy, a new addition, who doesn't seem to know what the hell to do. "Pippin!" my sister shouts, and the puppy burrows its head into the flank of one of the anvil-headed females, and there's more barking and some leaping.

"I'll probably just need to stay a week," I say. I drag my suitcase into the guest bedroom while she does her lion-tamer routine with the dogs and finally manages to slip inside and slam the door.

The last time I visited, three years ago, my husband and I tried unsuccessfully to sleep in this room; after an hour, he shoved me and said, "I'm suffocating, and my eyes are burning." We went out to the family room, where our son Jimmy was sleeping on the sofa, buried under two dogs. "Get up," we whispered, and he rose, complaining, and we drove to the Holiday Inn. This was when my sister had only two dogs and four cats.

"I'll empty the cat box every morning," she says now, and I say, "Oh, don't go to any trouble. I'll just use the toilet down the hall."

"Good one," she says. Then she tells me about Rex, cat number six, who lives in the guestroom closet and won't come out because the other animals bite and torment him. "He has an abscess and a leaky eye, poor thing." There are, I now notice, pieces of cat food and gravel all over the carpet, and a litter box at the foot of the bed. "Sorry about the smell," she says, though she doesn't sound sorry. "I mean, I don't even notice anymore."

I'm about to say that this is impossible, but then I realize I'm already starting to get used to it, too. If either Jimmy or Danny were speaking to me, this is what I would tell them: you can get used to pretty much anything.

•

Mel and I were prepared to eat mud and live with the beasts of the forest if that was what it took to find Bigfoot. "We'll build a fire with sticks," I said. "And eat wild strawberries." We'd been warned against the wild berries, but Mel had tried one and nothing happened to her. "I suppose we could eat snakes if we had to."

"I'm not eating snakes," Mel said. We were sitting on a small dirt island in the woods behind Maureen's house. We could see streaks of sky beyond the treetops. Our bare feet were coated in red dirt, so we washed them in the cold brown water and let the water bugs dance on our toes. It was a shiny Saturday afternoon in late August; cartoons were over for another week; school would start in ten days. Our kitchen table was stacked with Kmart bags of school supplies and crisp clothes with plastic tags in the collars. I would be starting fifth grade, and Mel would be in third.

"Listen," I said. We both held our breath and listened to the slow gurgle of water and the rustle and squawk of crows and jays. From somewhere, we heard a shrieking laugh, a car motor revving.

"It's him," said Mel. I wasn't sure if she meant Bigfoot or Maureen's stepfather. It was only a month earlier that we saw him with the turtles in his front yard. He'd pulled one from a box and put it on a wooden crate and then waved a stick until the jaws snapped down. "Watch this," Maureen had said, giggling, and we watched while he yanked until the neck came right off the turtle and blood spilled over the grass. He threw the head, with the stick still attached, into one plastic tub, and the body into another. "Isn't that great?" said Maureen. Beside me, Mel didn't say a word, and later that night she started crying at the dinner table, even though we were having cheese soufflé and not turtle soup.

"Would you rather eat toads or turtles?" I asked Mel as we dangled our feet in the water.

"Berries," she said, jabbing a twig into the dirt. "I'm eating berries. That's what Bigfoot eats."

"I don't think so," I said, but how did I know?

There was another shriek of laughter, which I recognized as Maureen's. I knew that if we stood up and walked over the dead tree and up the poison ivy hill, we would be able to see the deck that looked out over her plastic swimming pool. The last time I went to her house, we played hide and seek, and Maureen hid from me in the basement and didn't come out even when I hollered.

•

Mel, George, Amber and I eat dinner at the dining room table, all four of us crammed at one end because of the stack of papers and *National Geographics* and homeschool-schoolbooks on the other. The dogs whine downstairs, shut off by the baby gate; five cats watch us. "We cleaned off the table in your honor!" George says. George is about seven feet tall with a long ponytail. He's a musician and works in a Jiffy Lube. Amber has Mel's (and my) pasty skin, but she has George's black hair, so she looks like a character out of a British novel. She's ten and already wearing lipstick. Mel dresses like an Amish woman, in long sleeves and long skirts. All of her clothes are sturdy and stain-guarded.

Dinner is fake-meat lasagna; the fake-meat is gray and lumpy, like brains. "Interesting," I say. Nobody says anything. Amber is looking at me, chewing with her mouth open. I can tell that she's been instructed not to ask about her cousin Jimmy or her uncle Danny.

"I brought you a book," I tell her. I'm a middle school librarian, which means I spend a lot of time reading books to make sure they aren't full of sex and cussing. That's what the parents complain about. They don't complain about genocide or even about Grimm's fairy tales—the cut-off finger, the sliced-off heel, the murdering stepparents. But if someone drops an f-bomb, or if two boys kiss each other, watch out. "It's about animals."

"I just read *The Miracle Worker*," says Amber, and every-one relaxes now that we have something safe to talk about. "It was all right. And now I'm re-reading the first Harry Potter, but I haven't decided if I'm going to re-read *all* of them." She stares, bored, at her forkful of lasagna, then puts it down as if suddenly the world is too much for her. "May I be excused?" she says. "I'll take Tillie and Fiona for a walk. Pippin is my dog, and the other two are family dogs," she informs me. "We have to take Pippin by himself, because he doesn't obey yet."

"Are any of the cats yours?" I ask. "Or are they all family cats?"

"They're Mom's cats," she says. "But the fish and the parakeet belong to the family."

"What does Amber do for friends?" I ask when she's gone. Mel started homeschooling her last year when a seventh grader brought a handgun to school. She quit her job as a high school biology teacher, and George took on some extra work at another garage so they could make ends meet.

"She has friends," George says, a little defensively. "Her cousins Joey and Terry." Joey and Terry, I do not point out, are five years old.

"But, like, do kids come over?"

"No," says Mel. "I mean, the house is always a mess."

"Does she go over to anyone's house? Besides Joey and Terry?"

"There was that friend of hers, with the father who smoked pot," says George. "Amber came home and said, 'Jill's dad got kind of silly and he smelled funny.'"

"What the hell is wrong with people?" Mel says. And then she looks at me, and I know she's wondering what the hell is wrong with me, and why have I left my husband and son back in Maryland? I regret telling her about Jimmy setting his bedroom curtains on fire. "Accidentally!" I'd said. "You know how much he likes science."

"How is that science?" she'd asked.

"Did you ever tell Amber about Patches?" I ask now.

"Ugh, no," she says. "It would break her heart."

And all I can think is: Why hasn't it already been broken?

•

"What, were you raised by wolves?" our mother would say when we failed to accomplish some simple task like setting the table or cleaning our rooms. For some reason, I was the only one she hit—flat-palmed across the face, or across the rear with a hairbrush. My father hit me with a belt once, but then he cried and said he was sorry. He moved out soon after that.

"You could hit me, too, if you want," my sister said to our mother after she slapped me for not folding the napkins in diagonals.

"That's really nice of you, Mellie," our mother said, and kissed her on the forehead. "Go wash your hands."

•

After dinner, George opens a beer and offers me one, which I am grateful for. Mel settles down on the sofa with her iPad, and Amber, ruddy and smelling of outdoors, comes running up the steps in a frenzy of barking. One of the cats has settled in my lap; two others perch above me on the sofa. This house is nothing like the one Mel and I grew up in. Everything is soft and furry, literally, but all I can think is that there is a danger to this, too.

Amber is much too gentle-hearted, like my sister. Their hearts are made of cotton; stuffed full of it, like human teddy bears. The book I brought for her is one that arrived at the library by mistake, for children ages 6–10: *A Kid's Guide to Wild Nature.* There are photos of bears eating salmon, lions eating gazelles, toads eating bugs, and birds eating toads. Full color spreads. I think of telling her about Mel's python, the one her tenth-grade biology teacher gave her to take care of for a month. She tried to feed it anything but mice. Hamburger, cheese cubes. Ice cream. She let it roam free in the hallway between our bedrooms. Our twenty-year-old cat, Patches, didn't have a chance. When I came home from college for Thanksgiving, my mother was the one who told me what happened, adding, "Patches didn't suffer, but your sister cried for *weeks*."

I remember going outside and breathing in the cold, damp air. Since when did being strangled and swallowed by a python equal not-suffering? My father's car drove up—he was remarried, but he brought us a mincemeat pie every year. I thought of the woods between our house and Maureen Ray's, and I wished they hadn't been plowed down and turned into a development.

When I went back inside, I said, "Whatever happened to Maureen Ray?"

"Oh, her," said my mother. "Probably nothing very good."

•

Amber wants us all to go with her while she walks the new puppy, Pippin, around the block. "He still needs to learn basic commands," she tells me.

"Like stop being a maniac," says George. "No, thanks." He cracks open another beer.

"It's still too hot outside," says Mel. "Can we wait until it cools down some? Okay, boy, good boy," she adds, because Pippin has heard his name combined with the word *walk*, and he's barking and whining, his toenails scrabbling on the hardwood steps below the baby gate.

"See?" Amber says. "Now we *have* to take him. Leashy!" she says. "Who wants his leashy?"

All the dogs seem to really, really want their leashies, judging from the barking and drooling and jumping. Three of the cats scatter under furniture and two others jump up on the tattered sofa and begin to groom. "I'll go," I say. "I volunteer myself for this mission."

"Yay!" says Amber, and after she wrestles with the female dogs—"No! You girls had your turn!"—and forces a red leash around Pippin's frantic neck, we manage to get outside. From behind the closed front door I can hear my sister yelling above the barking, "Will you just cut it out? Give it a goddamn rest!"

"Come on, Pippin," says Amber. "You know where to go." He seems to want to go everywhere at once, but she yanks him toward the gravel road, the loop that goes up a hill and around the block. It's a quiet street with homes all built in the early 1980s, faded brick and big driveways. The air is humid; late August light cracks through the trees. Sprinklers sputter over lawns; a woman rises from her flower garden and lifts a hand in greeting. Something about the way she glares into the sun makes me think of my mother. I let my mother see Jimmy once a year, which I think is generous. My father is gone—one winter night five years ago, he wandered off and his wife found him shivering on a playground, and he died a week later. He should have been microchipped.

And I think of my own house, seven hours away: Jimmy's bicycle leaning against the screen door, the basketball net in the cul-de-sac where Jimmy patiently waits his turn with the other neighborhood kids. Danny turning hot dogs on the grill. Will they ever want me back?

"Do you have friends around here?" I ask Amber as we crunch over the gravel. We cross a tiny stream teeming with dancing water bugs. "Are there other kids your age?"

"Not really," she says, and I don't know if she means she doesn't have friends, or if there aren't any other kids. "When I grow up, I'm going to be a zookeeper. Did you know we have passes to the Mill Mountain Zoo, so we can go all the time? I have a member badge, and I'm going to volunteer there, and once I got to pet a goat."

"Wow," I say. "You sure do take after your mother."

She makes a noncommittal grunt to this, and tugs on Pippin's leash. "Sit!" she says to no effect. "Sit!"

"Can I try?" I ask, and Amber reluctantly hands over the leash.

"Run," I say, and Pippin and I take off as fast as we can, up the hill and around the bend, and now in the hazy distance I can just make out the Mill Mountain star on its hilltop. In an hour or so, when the sun sets, it will twinkle blue and red and yellow. Pippin is stronger and faster than he looks—still mostly wild animal, despite his cuteness; all instinct and momentum: *run, crap, eat, play, eat, crap, run run run.*

I run until I can't breathe, and then I let Pippin pull me further, until we're in a cul-de-sac dead end, both of us panting. Amber skips toward us, delighted. "Mom and Dad don't run!"

"Jimmy never wanted a pet," I manage to gasp, bent over, my side cramping.

"That's sad," says Amber. I hand her the leash. Pippin's tongue rolls with happiness, dollops of slobber splashing the pavement.

•

I cocooned myself in my bedroom for weeks after Danny took Jimmy to his mother's in Delaware. I called in sick for a few days, then I stopped calling. Danny found me swaddled in blankets, a tumbler of vodka beside my head. Everything soft. Everything furry.

I remember him tossing cold water on me. "Get up," he shouted, so I got up. I showered. I drank gulps of water from the sink. "I'm sorry," I said.

He told me he and Jimmy needed to move back in; school was starting soon. "Can you go somewhere else for a while?" Danny asked. "To your sister's for a week or two? I need to think."

I said I could. "I'm sorry," I said again.

"Don't turn into your mother," he said gently. "You need to be more civilized than that."

•

Mel and George are in the basement, which stinks worse than the living room, watching an angry chef curse at a skinny woman in a hairnet. "We love this show," Mel says. "How was your walk?" The female dogs are sprawled out panting, one on Mel, one on George; he maneuvers his beer around her thumping tail.

"It was good," I say.

"Aunt Helen ran up the hill," Amber says. "Then we ran back down. It was fun. Can we go again later? And then go tomorrow, after church?"

"We certainly can," I tell her. "I didn't know you all went to church." No one answers. A calico cat is staring at me from the top of the sofa. I can't keep track of any of their names. I think I can almost understand the appeal of being surrounded by so many creatures, human and animal. You feel warm, protected. Who needs religion? I find myself thinking of Maureen Ray: how when kids made fun of her—of her buck teeth, or her homemade dresses— she would close her eyes and shout, "Jesus loves me, Jesus loves me!" until they went away, or until the bus came, or until a teacher showed up and shook her.

"We don't go to church," I say. On TV, the chef is bleeping up a storm. "Jimmy can't seem to sit still." Amber looks at me. The calico steps carefully over my chest and another cat, white and fluffy, takes its place on the top of the sofa. "Also," I add, "nobody really seems to like it."

"I don't like it, either," says Amber.

"None of us like it," Mel snaps. "But we go anyway. It's what people do whether they want to or not."

"Like when we were little," I say, "and you would do puzzles the whole time, and I would just stare at cute boys. That's what I remember about church." And then at home, Mom would smack me for not setting the table correctly, or for not changing my shoes quickly enough, or folding the napkins wrong.

"Ha," bursts George, and I think he's going to say something about his own religious upbringing, but he points at the television and says, "Take that, you piece of shit walk-in freezer."

•

Jimmy is a small boy, too sensitive for his own good. The bullying started in second grade, mostly by a kid named Eddie who made fun of his buck teeth and later made fun of his braces, then his glasses. Then other kids got in on it: they called him four-eyes. Retard. They tripped him as he walked down the hall. He would get off the school bus crying. Danny and I talked to the principal, who said something along the lines of kids being kids.

So I taught Jimmy how to stand up to the people who hurt him. I didn't teach him to fight, just to say, "What the hell is your problem?" and "Don't take it out on me!"

"And whatever you do, don't cry," I said. "They love it when you cry."

He set his Batman curtains on fire one Saturday afternoon while Danny was running errands and I was making lunch. When the smoke alarm went off, I thought I was burning the grilled cheese. By the time Danny got home, Jimmy was sobbing in my arms, and I was telling him it was okay. I didn't smack him; I didn't even punish him. "It was an accident, right?" I said, and he said, "Right." I told Danny that we'd been doing an experiment that got away from us.

What I should have taught Jimmy is this: we all have rotten little cores in us, the capacity for pain, and also for cruelty. I think of mine as something shiny, like ore. Something hard and heavy and almost beautiful, and nothing— not even fire—can burn it out of me, or him, or anybody.

I didn't tell Danny that two days later I saw Jimmy knock down a disabled kid at the bus stop—just shove him over for no reason and then start to laugh, and all the other kids started laughing, too. I didn't tell Danny that I yelled for Jimmy to come inside, and that I hit him—hard, open-palmed—across the face, then sent him staggering back out to the bus stop. "Don't you dare cry," I told him. "They love it when you cry."

I know Jimmy would never have told Danny that I hit him—he knew he deserved it. But the guidance counselor saw the red mark, and Jimmy is an honest boy. The counselor called Danny.

●

I leave Mel, George, Amber, and the animals and go into the guestroom where my suitcase gapes on the chenille bedspread. There's a fresh turd in the cat box. "Rex?" I say. "Here, kitty kitty." I think I hear something shifting deep within the closet, but I'm not sure.

Mel enters the room in a riot of barking and shouting, and when she gets the door shut behind her she says, "Do you need anything? Another blanket?"

I tell her I don't. "I heard Rex in there," I say.

She sits down on the bed. "You'll never see him. He might come out when you're asleep."

"Remember Maureen?" I'm thinking of that last day we went Bigfoot hunting, how when we got close to Maureen's house, she came skipping out to meet us. She was wearing a pink ruffled bathing suit, a two-piece that made me understand that Maureen was older than me by at least a couple of years—that she was probably twelve, maybe even thirteen, even though she was my height. Usually she wore a baggy blouse and denim skirt, but now I could see that she had breasts, and hips, and that she was well aware of these assets.

"I got a bathing suit," she announced.

"I have a question for you," I said. "If Jesus loves you so much, why are you so ugly and stupid?"

Is it more or less terrible that I didn't actually mean to hurt her feelings? I just wanted to ask the question and see what would happen: set the fire and watch it burn. What happened was that she opened her mouth and stared at me. My sister gave a tiny gasp and ran back into the woods. Then Maureen began to cry, loud and wailing, and her stepfather came clattering down the wooden deck steps, and I took off as fast as I could go.

After that, she didn't invite us over to play with her Weebles Treehouse, or to see her stepfather make turtle soup. She ignored me at the bus stop, and once, I tried to make friends again by telling her I liked her dress, but she turned away. Later, I said hi to her when she was hugely pregnant, and I asked when she was due. "Soon," she said, and shrugged. And then she moved away. I thought I saw her sister once at Safeway, but it wasn't her.

"Ugh, Maureen," says Mel. "That was pretty gross, her stepfather getting her pregnant."

"What?" I say. "Her stepfather? How did I not know this?"

"Well, *obviously*. It was common knowledge. He went to jail."

"I don't think that happened," I say. "Are you sure?"

Mel shrugs. It occurs to me that my sister might understand more about the nastiness of the world than I do; then it occurs to me that George has probably gone through eight beers in the last three hours. I think of her yelling, "Give it a goddamn rest," and suddenly wonder who exactly she was talking to. I say, "I hit Jimmy, and now Danny wants to divorce me." I'm expecting Mel to be outraged, for her to storm off, maybe tell me to leave. But she shrugs again.

"Mom used to hit you all the time. That's what parents did."

"You don't," I point out.

"No," she agrees. "I could never do that."

When she leaves, I sit on the bed and listen. I can see Rex's tracks in the carpet, the little dents in the bowl of food where he pressed his nose. There's a new smattering of gravel next to the litter box. "I know you're there," I whisper. Outside the door, Pippin howls; the other two dogs whine and whimper. The humans turn off the TV and head up the stairs. Maybe Jimmy needs a pet after all, even if he doesn't want one: *Be gentle,* I could tell him, handing over Rex. *Be kind.* Maybe I can actually capture this cat, if I'm prepared to wait—until the dogs flop down, the parakeet goes quiet in his cage, the other five cats find their beds, the humans are snoring away. Until it's just me and Rex: two wild creatures wide awake in this dark house, wondering if the coast is clear.

The Sitters

Zena had named her girls Fluffy, Kitten, Boots, and Mopsy, but when baby number five turned out to be a boy, she didn't—as we all expected—call him Rocky, Rusty, Spike, or Snuggles. "His name is Barry," she said, kissing him on his smooth round head.

"Berry, like a fruit?"

"Barry, like a person."

We—the four babysitters of the neighborhood—took turns watching the children. They could be a handful, which was what we had learned was the polite term for lunatics. Some of us had other afterschool jobs, at McDonald's or Pizza Hut; some of us took ballet and tap; one of us was far too studious, worrying even her parents, who told her she should get out more. We went to the same school but traveled in different circles. Still, one thing we could agree on: Zena's daughters were a handful, but we adored Barry. Sometimes we would babysit together, two at a time, for half price, just to be able to tuck that smooth-headed boy into his crib and watch him sleep.

We didn't ask about the children's father—fathers? We didn't ask. We assumed that Kitten and Mopsy were full sisters because of their sharp noses, but then Kitten's nose grew more angular and Mopsy's soft and upturned, so we weren't sure anymore. When Zena first moved to town and advertised in the *Pennysaver* for "a sitter for four delightful daughters," Fluffy was a serious girl of eight, with chapped lips and two Shaun Cassidy singles she played over and over. Kitten, seven, was a shrieker; we joked that she would grow up to be an opera singer. She shrieked at spiders, at birds, at us. Boots was six, obsessed with cowboy movies. She galloped around the living room on a pretend horse, swinging her lasso, shooting her finger at the ceiling. She called us *pardner*, then stole from our purses. She gagged and tied up three-year-old Mopsy and left her under the kitchen sink until one of us heard her muffled sobs.

Mopsy was as soft as her name, sleepy and warm and chubby. You couldn't help but gnaw on her little toes, gum her little fingers while she laughed and kicked.

But Barry, even as a tiny baby, was different. We knew this, although our experience with babies was limited. His eyes flashed with preternatural knowledge, wide and calm and wise. It was as if he were forgiving us for all our sins: for losing our virginity behind the bleachers, for cheating on the American Government exam; for lying, and crying, and telling our parents we hated them. He was curious. He was skeptical. We remembered, later, those spoonfuls of Gerber carrots we flew into his open mouth—open up, here comes the airplane! How one day, just six months old, he said, "*Not* a plane." How he pointed to his toes and said, "*Not* piggies."

Zena, in our memory, was a whoosh of red dresses and sharp-heeled shoes. We could remember flowing hair— sometimes auburn, sometimes blonde. We remembered her Tic Tacs, her hi fi with the Barry Manilow records (though we refused to believe this was the silly reason behind baby Barry's name). We remembered her peeling off the dollar bills at the end of the evening. We remembered the refrigerator filled with . . . what was in that refrigerator? We couldn't remember after all. Wine coolers? No. Buttermilk? Perhaps. She was a nurse, or an orthodontist, or a schoolteacher, or a bus driver. When we asked our parents about her, they said, "Oh, who knows." They said, "She's a perfectly nice person." They never invited her to Christmas parties. We never saw her out in the world.

We saw her only in that square brick house with its three bedrooms, the air conditioner that chugged loudly in the summer, the black and white TV without a remote control. There was one bathroom, pink, with seashell towels. There were TV dinners and ice pops in the freezer (we remembered the freezer), and those were what we fed the children. Zena needed us only on Friday afternoons after school, and Saturday evenings, between seven and ten. She couldn't drive us home, of course—and leave the children entirely alone—but our fathers would come for us, pull up outside the house and honk—headlights glowing through the night. We couldn't remember our fathers ever coming inside.

We grew up, moved away, got married, divorced, had children or didn't. Sometimes on visits home, we'd wonder what happened to Zena and her children, and sometimes we'd drive by her house, but we never knocked. Fluffy would be old enough to babysit, we realized one day, and so would Kitten, Boots, Mopsy—and finally it occurred to us that all the children were old enough to be on their own.

Except for Barry, who stayed a baby in our minds for years—until one of us was home for a funeral and saw the newspaper article about his high school valedictorian speech/exposé that led to the principal's firing. She gasped, and tears of delight sprang to her eyes. She said, *I must tell the other sitters.*

We had fallen out of touch, but she found us on Facebook and told us the news, and we all began to follow Barry's career: from Ivy League rabble rouser to amateur sleuth, to (and we no longer needed the local paper to keep track of him) famous debunker of faith healers, politicians, and vitamin supplements. We watched him on talk shows, admired his height and his teeth and his loud, angry laugh. And when we heard him announce that he would be appearing in his own hometown, at the new arena, we made arrangements.

We booked hotels and rental cars, and we met—for the first time in almost forty years, all four of us sitters together again—in the lobby, in front of the concession stands and the Barry DeBunker T-shirt displays. We laughed and hugged; some of us were larger than we used to be, some were smaller. Two of us had nearly died from different diseases, one of us had a semi-famous rock star daughter. We stood in a circle and chatted about our lives, then grew silent as it dawned on us that we still had nothing in common but Zena's children. One of us drifted off to buy a T-shirt for her nephew.

We never could recall who recognized the woman first—perhaps it happened to all of us at once. She was wearing a white hat and a red, ankle-length gingham dress that seemed too flimsy for the winter season. Her shoes were flat and black, and her hair was auburn and twisted across her head like a woman in a story we could barely remember. Maybe we said it in unison: *Boots.*

She looked over, and her eyes went wide. She gave a shy smile. She was holding up a T-shirt and she set it back on the display and came over to say hello, thrusting out her hand very formally to each of us in turn.

"You're back," we said.

"I never left," she replied. Then she blushed. "Well, for a while I did." And she told us how she had stayed with her mother as her sisters left, one by one, until it was just her and Barry and their mother in that square brick house. And then Barry—who would have thought? Such a genius, he practically sprouted wings and flew out of the house and into the stratosphere. She and Zena led a quiet life; Boots got a job as a waitress in a new chain of restaurants, and Zena retired from her bus driving job when her knees went bad. They didn't go out much but played quiet board games and ate quiet meals at home. When her mother grew feeble and blind, Boots read to her from the same books we'd read to her and her siblings. Sometimes her sisters swept in for a brief visit; sometimes her brother sent an envelope of money.

When Boots was thirty-seven, her mother died quietly in her sleep, and the day after the funeral, a bearded cowboy broke down in his Land Rover just outside the house. It was love at first sight.

"How wonderful," we said.

They married and moved to a northern country we'd never heard of and built a small cabin in the wilderness. We could picture it as she talked: the glistening snow, the ice crystals. They built fires and they hunted in the forest, and Boots befriended and tamed a small fox. It burrowed between them as they slept; it rode high on her curlers as she did the chores. They had no children, but it was a beautiful life, until one day her husband went out during an early thaw and she heard the echoing crack of the ice all the way across the field. By the time she reached him, it was too late. It wasn't a sudden death; she managed to haul him to shore. But he had amnesia and no longer recognized her, and he never would again, and three weeks later he died shivering in her arms, and then even the fox ran away.

"So here I am, back again," she said. "And isn't it marvelous about Barry."

We didn't know what to say. We wanted to hug her, but we didn't. Her sisters, she told us, lived in cities and worked in offices. She didn't offer more. Her hair sat crooked on her head, and we realized it was a wig. We remembered her mother's hair, blonde one day and auburn the next. All fake.

She disappeared into the line of people heading into the arena. After a moment, we filed in, too. Our seats were too far back for us to see anything clearly, but we applauded when our little Barry made a spoon levitate and cured a faith healer of faith healing, and made an elephant think it was a mouse. For the grand finale, he revealed that what we'd thought, through the sheer power of suggestion, was a new arena in our town, was in fact an old barn in an old field. The walls vanished before our eyes and we followed the crowd, blinking, to find our cars lined up in a pasture.

There was no sign of Boots. We didn't wait around for an autograph.

We took our separate cars to a café on Main Street. We drank tea. One of us had wine. We talked about the stories we'd told the children as they grew up, the books we'd read to them: one of us read the book about Foxy the Tame Fox; another read of pioneers and cracking ice; another of handsome, bearded princes from northern countries. One of us blushed, remembering all the amnesia victims in the soap operas she'd loved to watch.

We thought of young Boots, with her lasso and her galloping, and how she had said her brother's name with such longing and sadness that we first mistook it for the word that means to inter under the earth.

One of us started to cry.

One of us dared to say, "She's there, right now. You know she is. In that little house, all alone."

No one spoke. There was nothing we could do, was there? Nature, nurture, heredity, mystery. We didn't raise her—not entirely. We thought of the pink bathroom. We thought of the old books and the old TV and the refrigerator. Outside, darkness had fallen across the town we had moved away from and barely thought of, even in dreams. It was getting late, we said. We gave each other hugs. We gathered our purses, then texted our loved ones to let them know we were on our way home.

Starry Night

"I guess we're supposed to feel something," Patricia says, staring at a Van Gogh painting of the Rhône as they stand next to the Rhône.

"Or think something," Charles corrects gently.

"Well, I think I feel hungry," she says.

They are, as the walking tour brochure has promised in five languages, *following in the footsteps of Van Gogh*. All over Arles there are easels of Van Gogh paintings in front of the things they depict: in front of the night café, for instance, which was full of tourists this afternoon under the yellow awning. Or now, *Starry Night Over the Rhône*. "Such lovely lights on the water," Patricia says, trying to muster up something in the way of awe. This is difficult partly because it's a clammy summer day, and partly because of the crowd of loud American students disembarking from a nearby bus.

"Well, you can't get away from tourists in a tourist town," Charles says, ducking a bearded boy's outstretched iPhone.

Since when are you an expert on tourist towns? Patricia does not say. Neither of them has been to Europe before, or even west of the Mississippi River. She had thought they would fumble their way through France together, two sixty-something-year-olds out in the world, but Charles took the guidebook from her somewhere over the Atlantic and never relinquished it. She has let him lead her through the South of France for four days now—Marseille, Aix-en-Provence, Avignon, and now Arles; when she asks to see the map or the guidebook, he tells her, "Just stick with me." So far, so good, she supposes. They've maneuvered (*he's* maneuvered, she's followed) taxis, the TGV station, and the bus from Avignon. Still, she feels a little like a blind person with a guide dog.

The twenty or so students have tossed their bags and sketch pads on the ground and congealed into photo-taking clumps. "Excusez-moi," says a goateed boy and nudges Patricia away from the easel painting so he can pose next to it, hands on his hips, pouting at the sky.

According to Wendy, Patricia's daughter, "France will open your hearts and minds to the layers of the past," but Patricia is still waiting for this to happen. What layers? Whose past? Certainly not her own. On the bus, they had passed IKEAs and supermarkets and McDonald's, but there was no other word for it all except foreign. Nothing that reminded her of the Florida landscape of her youth, or the Virginia horse farms and strip malls of her current life. She'd been surprised by the gray-green and yellow mountains. Everything seemed so baked and parched. And then the shocking blue of the Mediterranean, after the grimy alleys of Marseille. So much bright sun; the smell of all those flayed fish by the docks.

The trip is a twentieth anniversary present from Wendy and her husband Ben, "because you and Charles never do anything interesting," as Wendy phrased it. Patricia had protested: What about terrorists, what about kidnappings and general crime? The world was so unstable. "And you should wait until when?" Wendy said. "Until you're dead?" She and Ben are literature professors and have very strong ideas about what is and isn't interesting. Travel is interesting. Church is not interesting, except in the most disturbing of ways. "Most popes were awful, corrupt people," Wendy informed her mother. "So be sure to keep that in mind when you're in Avignon." "But I'm Methodist," Patricia reminded her, and Wendy said, "*All* religion is just a way of repressing people. You shouldn't even go to church."

Well, thought Patricia, annoyed, look who's trying to repress *whom*. She and Charles met at church after their twenty-year-marriages and then divorces from their high school sweethearts. Marrying the high school sweetheart was "such a cliché," Wendy said. Neither Patricia, nor Charles, nor their first spouses had known it was a cliché. It was just what people did.

"I'm still fucked up from last night," a girl in a butt-length skirt is saying. "Is it uncouth to barf in the river?"

There seems to be someone in charge of these boisterous, barely-clad students: a small, furry man of early middle age, who's waving and shouting, "Follow me, please!" and heading up the river bank. A barge slides through the flat brown water. When the students have gone, Patricia realizes that Charles is gone, too—or no, there he is on an iron bench, his skinny legs crossed, hunched over as if he's in pain.

"Honey?" says Patricia. He seems much older than his sixty-five years, and when he looks up and squints at her— he's forgotten his sunglasses—she has the odd thought that he's forgotten where he is. Then she realizes he's holding his phone in both hands.

"I'm posting to Facebook," he calls. "Give me a minute."

•

This was a surprise: your spouse of twenty years can turn into a completely different person once you set foot in a foreign country. Why was that? For instance, she didn't know that Charles—normally so reserved at home—would turn out to be one of those people who speaks too loudly in restaurants. Or that he would persist in his remedial

French-speaking even when the waiters switched to English to try and make him stop. Or that he is suddenly so savvy about social media. They still have an answering machine on their landline at home.

And Patricia had not known, until now, that she is a souvenir hog, unable to resist even one bright-awninged shop, one rack of postcards featuring lavender and kittens. Her suitcase is already stuffed with bags of herbs and with T-shirts (for Wendy and Ben's daughter and Charles' two grandsons) and souvenir spoons. Her grandmother had collected those, and Patricia and her sister had used them to perform fake psychic experiments that involved bending them out of shape on their noses. And now she has three ridiculous spoons herself: Marseille, Avignon, Arles. "They're small," she said to Charles, as if this was enough reason to buy something useless.

•

Every restaurant is overflowing with tourists—their shopping bags, their laughing voices—but eventually Patricia and Charles find a small, nearly-empty café tucked in an alley behind the Roman amphitheatre. It had shocked her, this ancient coliseum smack in the middle of the town she'd assumed was famous only because of its famous painter. It was one thing to hear Charles' commentary—"The amphitheatre is almost two thousand years old," he intoned, as if he hadn't just read it in the Rick Steves guidebook—and another to see it rising up before you, making you think of gladiators and lions.

A woman in a black dress briskly leads them to a table next to the window under two oil paintings: one of a bull fighter wielding a red cape, the other of a woman who seems to be wearing a knotted doily on her head. Neither of the paintings appears to be a Van Gogh, and Patricia feels a twinge of pride at knowing at least this much. She retrieves a stack of postcards from her purse. "I'm going to post things the old-fashioned way," she says, and then, "Oh, hello!" to the frowning waiter who has manifested beside their table. Back home in Virginia, she loves chatting with wait staff, but here she feels shy and foolish.

"*Oohn carafe* of rosé," Charles says to the waiter, who says, "Of course," in perfect, snobby English.

"I don't really like rosé," Patricia informs Charles for the third or fourth time, glancing up from her postcard. She has written *Greetings from Arles!* even though that's what it says on the front of the postcard, in bright purple, over a photo of a kitten holding a paintbrush.

"Oh, but the rosé is so crisp and lovely here," comes a woman's voice from behind Patricia. "Nothing like that swill you get back home." She is sitting by herself at a small round table: a woman of about Wendy's age, wearing a lime-green cloche hat. She has a square, smiling face—the kind of face Patricia's mother might have called handsome. There is *oohn carafe* of rosé in front of her, and a steaming plate of indeterminate meat. She raises her wine glass. "Cheers to fellow travelers from distant lands."

"Virginia," says Charles. He's scooted his chair out from the table. Patricia, her neck in a cramp from craning around, says, "Oh, hello."

"Maryland!" says the woman. "How nice."

What's nice, exactly? But Charles also seems to find it nice, because he's saying, "Please join us, won't you?" Charles, who refuses to answer the doorbell at home, who sits so silently through family gatherings that Wendy had taken Patricia aside once to ask, "Do you think he's deaf?"

The woman's name is Mary, and she's traveling by herself because her husband is too busy being a French professor to join her. "So I said, I'll just go alone, why not?"

"Good for you!" says Charles.

The woman seems, in Patricia's limited knowledge of such things, a little bit drunk. Something about the way she laughs and the brightness in her eyes—and, yes, the nearly empty carafe of wine that she finishes off with a smack of the lips. "Please," says Charles, "have some of ours." Mary offers them bites of her meal—"It's bull stew. *Taureau.*"—holding out a fork to Charles as if he's a baby. "Open up," she says. To Patricia's amazement, he does.

"None for me, thanks," she tells Mary's advancing fork. She tries to smile around the tart, horrible wine.

"No, but you should," Mary says and waves the waiter over so Charles can point to her plate and announce, holding up two fingers, "*Duh.*"

•

Two days before Patricia and Charles left for France, Wendy called to inform her that Lawrence—Wendy's father, Patricia's high school cliché sweetheart—was publishing a book of poems "with an actual, reputable press. Isn't that *amazing?*" She waited.

"Poems?" Patricia said at last.

"It's poems, not *poimes.* There's one up online already, as sort of a preview. I'll send it to you."

"I had no idea," was all Patricia could think to say. She supposed she wasn't terribly surprised. Lawrence: he never ran out of words, and that was the thing she had first loved about him, the way he would fill every silence with a story or a fact. In senior world history class, everyone had given fifteen-minute presentations, but he had gone on for an hour—the entire class period!—about the Industrial Revolution. "Lawrence," the teacher said when the bell rang, "would you like to continue your presentation tomorrow?" He did. And the next day, too.

Later, he'd gone into the ministry; she taught fourth grade. They moved from Orlando to Maryland to Roanoke. Wendy came along; then William—who died at four months. The doctors had no explanation, no words except "I'm sorry for your loss." Patricia kept going to church; Lawrence quit the ministry and went into advertising. Eventually, on the rare occasions when they saw each other, they were having two different conversations at the same time, which infuriated them both so much that they kept on talking, louder and louder, until one of them slammed out the door.

And so Charles was a revelation, his stinginess with words. Patricia found pleasure in prying out each shy opinion, each morsel of his history: his alcoholic father, his first wife's depression, his sons' brushes with the law. She was, as she'd discovered after leaving Lawrence, an extrovert after all, once she wasn't crushed by the weight of Lawrence's conversation. She talked to strangers in supermarkets, to wait staff and cashiers; she welcomed new church members with cookies and stayed for hours in their living rooms, chatting and chatting. "Does Charles have any friends?" Wendy once asked, and Patricia had to think for a very long time. "*I'm* his friend," she said. They watched two episodes of Miss Marple every night before bed. They sat together in their living room overlooking the bird feeder and Patricia talked and talked, and Charles always seemed—even if he was leafing through a book or clicking on his iPad—to be listening.

•

Mary is saying, "It's not that I should have *expected* him to want to come with me. You get used to not expecting things from people—first my mother went crazy, and then my dad died."

Please stop talking, Patricia thinks. She nods and places her fork on top of her half-eaten stew. It's too rich; her stomach queases. The wine is almost gone, and her head feels swaddled in cotton. Outside the window, she can see the American students traipsing up the steps of the amphitheatre to pose, sweaters tied around their tiny waists. A black and yellow cat picks its way across a stone wall. *Look, a cat*, she almost says to Charles—but he's leaning toward Mary, nodding.

"My husband is a very good man," she's saying, "but he already has his five kids, you know? From three different wives? Hard to compete with that." She laughs. "Not that I'm competing. And I certainly don't want to divorce him, because that would be so lonely." She looks at Patricia, then Charles, and seems about to ask them something.

Patricia clears her throat. "Charles, should we walk to . . . what's next on the tour? The hospital?"

"The hospital!" Mary cries. "It's fantastic. The courtyard's been renovated so it looks just like the painting. You can go up and stand where Vincent did when he painted it."

Vincent, as if they're friends. Well, thinks Patricia a little cruelly, maybe they would have been.

"It's been so great talking to you both," Mary says. Her eyes look a little swimmy, her hat askew.

"You, too," says Charles. His eyes seem a little swimmy, too, behind his glasses. "Where are you off to next?"

"Well." She leans back in her chair. "Tomorrow I'm going to Aix, then Nice. Maybe Monte Carlo. I don't know. I'm sorry." She flaps at her face with her hands. "I've had too much wine."

Patricia tugs on Charles' sleeve, like a child. The waiter swoops through and scoops their euros off the table, calls, "*Bonne journée,*" over his shoulder.

But Charles, instead of standing, says, "We almost didn't get here. To this town."

Mary blinks at him. Patricia says, "We can't keep Mary here all day."

"We're staying in Avignon," Charles goes on. "Which is what? Twenty minutes from here?" He looks at Patricia, who shakes her head. "Something like that. But this morning, Patricia asks the front desk person—young guy, speaks English—when does the bus leave for Arles?"

"Oh," says Patricia, gathering her purse on her lap, "this is not very interesting."

"And he says, 'What? Where?' '*Ahrl,*' Patricia says. And he says, 'I'm sorry, but I have no idea where that is.'"

Patricia is clutching her purse. Hearing Charles say this out loud makes her face burn. She had thought the man was playing a trick on her, that she was—in some mysterious way—being swindled, duped. It had even occurred to her that Wendy had set her up to make a fool of herself.

Charles is lurched forward in his chair. "So then I take out my map and point, and he says—" Charles is laughing, Mary is laughing. "Oh, Ach. *Ach!*"

"There's an r sound in there," Patricia protests.

"And we get to the bus station. I'm ready to go to the ticket window, but Patricia says no, let her do it." *I wanted to be brave,* Patricia wants to say—to explain—but Charles is still barreling on. "She says, like a question, *Ach?* And of course, the ticket person just laughs at her. She's standing there, saying, Ach? *Ach?* Like she's choking to death."

Mary's face is pinched into a red howl. She slaps her hand on the table. And Charles, too, is convulsed with laughter, caught up in the pleasure of telling a story to a stranger; that the story makes Patricia seem like an idiot doesn't matter, or that the waiter and the lady in the black dress are giving them warning looks. Outside, the students are walking up the street, around the corner of the alleyway, their shouts like rocks against the window.

Patricia thinks of Charles turning to her before their plane took off, his face gray, saying, "I've never been on a plane before." She'd laughed at that: "You've never been on a *plane?*" That's something Mary might find amusing. Holding one's tongue, Patricia thinks. Now there's an image for one of Lawrence's poems: a moist, palpating creature in your palm, longing to send out a call to the entire world.

•

Patricia follows Charles through the sunlight into the flowering courtyard of the yellow hospital, its walls and archways the color of pale meringue against the flat blue sky. A round fountain burbles in the center of bright topiary—

red, green, pink flowers and shrubbery sliced into neat tri-
angles by stone walkways. "We can go up the steps to the
balcony and see the easel," says Charles. He yawns. "If you
want." As if on cue, the American students appear, traipsing through the courtyard with their phones outstretched.
They disappear under an archway and reappear a moment
later above Patricia and Charles, their laughter pouring out
into the air. "Lend me your ear!" someone yells.

"I think," says Patricia, "they're following in the footsteps of *us*. But no, I've seen enough."

The wine and the sun have made her sleepy. Her knee
was replaced last year but it still throbs; and now her other
knee is aching, too. One breast gone to cancer; a hearing
device in her left ear; a new knee. Charles has had a shoulder replaced, a cancerous mole scraped from his back.
"We're lucky, though," she said one night, as they tucked
their scarred bodies into bed. Their parents had died in
their sixties, from heart attacks and cancers: "The usual
suspects," as Wendy said once with a shuddering sigh. This
trip, Patricia has come to realize, is not so much a gift for
an anniversary as for an entire life: *You will die soon*, Wendy
is saying. *And your world is too small.*

No, it's not, Patricia thinks, as she gathers postcards
from a spinning rack under the shadow of a yellow archway. Beside her, Charles is poking at his phone.

"Who's reading your posts?" Patricia asks.

He looks up. "The boys. Wendy. And Lawrence."
He looks back down, keeps poking at the buttons. "I'm
explaining that we're at the hospital where Van Gogh came
in 1888 after he cut off his ear."

"Okay," says Patricia. So now he cares what Lawrence
thinks?

She hasn't told Charles about Lawrence's book of
poems. The men met a few times, cordially, at family gatherings. There were brisk handshakes before they drifted
to separate rooms. Charles spent thirty years repairing air

conditioners, and Lawrence went from advertising to psychology to, apparently, poetry. She certainly doesn't think Charles will be jealous about Lawrence's book, but he might be curious. He might, out of politeness, buy a copy — or at least read that horrible poem that was posted online about the King Tut exhibit Lawrence and Patricia and nine-year-old Wendy had gone to at the Smithsonian in 1977. He'd practically swooned over those gods and goddesses and ivory jars with shriveled body parts. What Patricia remembers most about that exhibit is looking away from a winged alabaster woman and realizing that Wendy was gone. She'd run panicked through the dim-lit rooms, calling for her daughter, finally finding her frowning at a glass case of mummified cats.

But there's no mention of this in Lawrence's poem. It's called "Valley of the Kings," and it's about the breakdown of a marriage, even though — as far as Patricia is concerned — the marriage hadn't started to break down yet. Sometimes an ivory jar of shriveled internal organs is just a jar of organs, she wants to tell him. Sometimes a king in a golden sarcophagus is just a boy who died.

•

They take the five o'clock train back to Avignon; she lets Charles buy the tickets, watches him compose whatever he's composing on his phone as the bright trees and clay-roofed houses slide past the window. His silences have, in recent years, begun to exasperate her. At the Petit Palais yesterday, they had checked their umbrellas and wandered through room after room of gold-haloed madonnas and children. "Beautiful," she had murmured in room one. Charles said nothing. By room nine, she was feeling dizzy: so *many* madonnas, their faces blank and pink; the Jesuses with faces of tiny old men, clawing toward a nipple. "How painful," she said then, fighting back the urge to cry or shout, waiting for him to say, "What's painful?" even though she'd have no answer; but Charles said, "The Botticelli in room eleven was painted in 1467."

"I pronounced it the way Wendy said it," she tells him now, as he snaps a photo out the train window.

He turns to her. "What?"

"You know." She turns away, feeling ridiculous. Let it go, she thinks. "Never mind."

•

She had tried to refuse Wendy's gift. "A tour of New England is more our style," she'd said.

"Why are you such a coward?" Wendy demanded. "You've never left the country. Don't you have any curiosity?"

Patricia would never have agreed to this trip if Wendy hadn't been so rude about it. How was that for a life lesson: the behavior that got you punished in your childhood (*No ice cream if you don't apologize!*) would make your mother bow to pretty much any demand when you were both older. *Be less like yourself and more like me,* Wendy had said, which is of course what all children say to their parents. *Want what I want: ice cream, Disney World, a world with no baths.* And later: *trips to Europe. Cars with less gas consumption. Vote for Democrats. Read my father's poems and find them wonderful. Live forever.*

Lawrence never remarried—something Patricia finds sad—but he has been to Japan, Russia, Kenya. A Fulbright to India. Wendy met Ben on a Fulbright to Italy. "Maybe I'm just full-dumb," Patricia had said once and was surprised by how awful that made her feel.

She and Wendy had worked out a compromise: six days instead of two weeks. The South of France instead of a tour of Paris, Rome, and Madrid. "It's very important to me," Patricia said to Charles, who nodded once and said, "Well, then we'll go." The next day, they went to the post office to apply for passports, handing over birth certificates and tiny square photos that made them both look pale and stunned.

●

The afternoon light is thickening when they arrive back in Avignon and walk through the medieval city walls. The tree-canopied boulevard that leads through the city, to the Palace of the Popes and the river beyond, is loud with café chatter and the honking of tiny cars. Charles pauses at an ATM, pokes his bankcard in the slot. Patricia gazes toward the pedestrian mall where they'd eaten lunch yesterday — the Place Something-or-Other — despite Charles' warning that the cafés there were overpriced tourist traps. The steak was chewy, the fries soggy, and Patricia felt almost embarrassed to have enjoyed them so much. Charles read to her from the guidebook while Patricia watched a woman arrange flowers outside the window: sunflowers and lilacs and floppy white roses.

As if reading her thoughts, Charles says, "Tonight we'll eat someplace authentic." He tucks his wallet back into his pocket.

"What's *not* authentic?" Patricia says. She spreads her arms, almost knocking into a woman striding past on the pavement. "Here we are. In France. French traffic, French trees, French cars. It's as authentic as it gets." She feels shaky with annoyance. Tell me something real, she wants to say, even though she has no idea what this might mean.

But Charles doesn't say a word. He takes her hand, and she lets him lead her away from the boulevard and through the narrow, cobbled streets to their hotel. For some reason she almost expects to see Mary, walking alone in her silly hat — alone, yes, but not divorced. Divorce: that's a country you want to pass through as quickly as possible, full of strange customs, with a currency and language that make no sense. During those seven years between Lawrence and Charles, Patricia had dated three men — one a widower, one divorced, one never married. She had let the widower kiss her once, and when he fell toward her on her front step, she realized he was drunk—had been drunk all evening—and shoved him away. She let him drive himself home.

At the hotel, the proprietor is busy talking to a young couple with three blue suitcases lined up behind them; Patricia follows Charles up the cramped steps to their room on the third floor. She pulls open the window, and the curtains stir a little in the breeze. Outside: an alley lined with pale yellow buildings; a rectangle of periwinkle sky above the clay rooftops.

Charles has collapsed on the bed, one arm flung over his eyes. "I'm so tired," he says.

"Old age," says Patricia. "Now there's a place we never expected to find ourselves." Charles grunts. "The souvenirs are crap," she says. "But the locals are generally kind."

Tomorrow, they will take the train back to Marseille and spend one last night there. Then, the plane back home. Already, everything is blurring together in her memory—sunlight, green awnings, yellow buildings, carousels.

"We should tell Wendy about *Ach*," Patricia says, astonishing herself. "Or you can tell it; I'll do the sound effects." She grips herself around the neck, makes some gagging noises.

"Really?" Charles smiles weakly

"Maybe you can tell them I mimed chopping off an ear." She demonstrates.

"Everything aches," Charles says. His face looks pinched.

"Don't think about that," she tells him. She does a karate chop next to her ear. "*Ach*," she says, thinking: Maybe Lawrence will write a damn poem about it. And he will, or at least he'll try. Most of it will be about the loneliness of foreign travel, and that will take him on a jaunt through a metaphor about rivers and history, his own childhood in Florida. He will show it to Patricia, and she will tell him, "It's very nice."

A small breeze lifts the curtains of their room—a room in a building which is, according to Charles, over five hundred years old—in an ancient town, an even older country, across thousands of miles of ocean from the country they have lived their entire lives—the place where they will eventually pass out of the world completely. She thinks of the bird feeder in their yard, the finches and cardinals. Now, nighttime sounds filter up to them: a distant bus, the snap of heels. Voices speaking in a language she must be content not to know, any more than she needs to know exactly how far the light of the stars has traveled to reach her.

In the Museum of Tense Moments

I tell my daughter I'm taking her to the new museum as a birthday present.

"But what if I don't want to go?" she asks. "What if I want another Bot Buddy for my birthday present?"

"You'll like it," I say. "And you don't need another Bot Buddy."

Of course, I'm not sure she'll like it. It might be too soon to go; the museum is so new, the crowds are still terrible, there are still kinks to work out. The average Tripadvisor rating is only three stars. It's expensive. Also, maybe Sarah is too young; she just turned eleven. The museum is intended for older audiences—but not *too* old. You have to sign a waiver promising not to sue if you have a heart attack or suffer from "emotional distress."

"All the cool kids are going," I say. "The high school kids."

This is true. You see them around town in their MTM T-shirts, which feature a big bloodshot eyeball and the slogan *I'm Not Telling.*

Sarah is going through a difficult stage, spending too much time in her room with Naomi—her Bot Buddy—and her VR animals. She works on a virtual ranch she designed when she was seven with her VR father before the Glitch.

She stays up late feeding tigers and roaming the camp with her rifle, stalking a shadowy bandit that steals eggs and sets fires. Her teachers report that she's intelligent but unmotivated. Instead of thought-waving with other kids she just watches movies on her finger screen. She made Naomi punch another kid's Bot Buddy and denied it, even when there were goggles and replays everywhere record- ing it.

I tried to tell her stories of my own childhood, the things I'd endured, my own loneliness. And look, I turned out fine! But we don't seem to share the same language. I told her how I used to carry a phone device in my pocket or in my purse, how I had to send text messages to people to know what they were doing. And her grandmother— wow, she had to wait by the phone for a boy to call her. It was a plastic machine, I told Sarah, and it hung on the wall with a long curly cord, and it rang when someone wanted to talk to you.

She said, "I have no idea what any of that means," and then clamped her VR set on and went off to hunt the bandit.

•

You have to deactivate all of your screens, and Bot Buddies aren't allowed past the cloak room. The line begins a block away. A cold rain is spitting down, and we shiver in our coats. I'm glad I made Sarah wear her boots. We haven't been to the city in almost a year, not since we last visited her VR father in his mid-town loft. I designed him myself. He played the piano and the trumpet. He told jokes. He said, *Atta girl.* I gave him a face like a friendly lion and hair like a twentieth-century rock star. He wore skinny ties and chinos and had big yellow paws. He was perfect, and Sarah loved spending time with him, but when the Glitch hap- pened, he was deactivated. I never got around to reformat- ting him.

"Are you nervous?" I ask Sarah, as we shuffle toward the entrance.

"A little," she says. The other people in line are in their thirties, forties, and older; a few give us disapproving glances, and one woman says, "This is no place for a child." But the scanner beeps Sarah and me green as we enter, and I feel vindicated—especially when I see the scoldy woman beep red and be taken aside by Nurse Bots for extra Health and Wellness scanning.

The marble hallway opens to a set of eight rooms, and the crowds stream into them, disappearing into more rooms, and more. There are no Bot Docents; there is no map.

"I guess just start anywhere," I say.

"I wish Naomi was here," Sarah mumbles as we follow a line of people into a brightly lit room. "What is *that*?"

"It's a bench," I say. "And an old man."

Because that's what it is. A green wooden bench, the kind you used to see in parks. And a white-haired man in black trousers, a tattered blue windbreaker. His face is both gray and yellow. He's hunched, staring into space.

"What's he *doing*?"

"He's sitting."

"Ohhh, he's a Povvy."

I forgot that she even knew about Povvies. They were pretty much swept out of the country a decade ago.

We watch as a young woman in blue jeans and a turtle-neck sweater walks into the exhibit. She has long dark hair pulled back in a ponytail.

"Hey," the man calls. "Pretty lady."

"Oh no," says Sarah.

There's some shoving behind us, and a man whispers, "God, I hated Povvies."

"You got any change?" the Povvy shouts, but the woman ignores him, walking past, looking straight ahead. "So I can buy a meal? I just want a meal."

"No," the woman says, and then another glass door swings open and she walks up to a window that says ICE

CREAM and hands a piece of paper to a man in a paper hat.

"That's money," I tell Sarah, and she says, "I know that."

The old man is walking toward the woman with the ice cream. "I saw you," he says. "I see you. You said you didn't have any money, but you did. You too good to talk to me?"

"Let's move on," Sarah says, so we follow a stream of people into the next room, where three suitcases churn around on a conveyor belt while a woman and her tiny son stand next to it, gripping each other's hands. All the suitcases are marked NOT YOURS.

"They don't have their stuff," I explain to Sarah. "And there's nothing they can do about it."

"Huh," says Sarah.

We make our way through more rooms: there's a teenage boy sitting on a single bed, staring at a phone—"See, it's one those old ones," I tell Sarah—picking up the handset, putting it back down again. Picking it up.

In another room: a dining room table with six people eating silently, not making eye contact. Two sputtering red candles on the table, a turkey carcass.

"Who are those people?" Sarah whispers, and I say, "I think it's a family."

I'm starting to think it's all getting through to her: the ways the world used to work, all the opportunities for missed connections and miscommunication and misunderstandings and helplessness. We hurry past blue flashing lights; past small children holding out candy bars. A man with a clipboard, calling, "Just a moment of your time."

A woman sits by herself at a restaurant table and stares at her wristwatch, a concept I once tried to explain to Sarah. Then she takes out a phone device and starts pushing its buttons.

"She can't use thought-wavers to find out where her friend is," I say. "She has to try to find her with that phone, using words. But her friend isn't answering."

"Is her friend *dead?*" Sarah asks, her eyes wide.

"Maybe. But the woman won't know it until later."

"Ohhh," says Sarah.

"Do you see how easy it is for you?" I tell her. "You have it so easy."

She doesn't say anything.

We enter a room strung with crepe streamers, a disco ball twirling from the ceiling. A girl Sarah's age sits by herself in a chair while a group of boys stands nearby laughing. One of the boys keeps looking at the girl. When he looks away, she looks at him. There's a window behind them, rain slanting in bright shards through the night sky.

"It's a middle school mixer," I explain. "He wants to dance with her, and she wants to dance with him, but they don't have thought-wavers or finger screens."

"I can't stand this," Sarah says. "I want to leave."

I watch the boy drift over to the girl. "It's *beautiful,*" I murmur, but Sarah has already turned away. She's staring at her fingers even though the screens are deactivated.

"This isn't even a real museum," Sarah says, loud enough that several people stop and look. "I want Naomi and my animals. I want to catch the bandit before he burns down another fence."

I watch the boy and girl staring at each other, their faces flushed and terrified. The last time I felt this way was when Sarah was still a baby, before the screens and the lion-father, when my heart was like that glittering ball twisting just out of reach, suspended and cracked open. Maybe now is the time to tell Sarah that the bandit is me: that I'm keeping an eye on her, tiptoeing through her animal kingdom and setting small, harmless fires. I open the traps and let the wild rats roam free. Sometimes I'm a snake slithering just out of sight.

I turn to tell her how proud I am of her, that I'll buy her whatever she wants in the gift shop. "This wasn't so bad, was it?" I say.

But she's gone.

Maybe she'll come back, or maybe she'll find her way to the exit, and the doors, and the world beyond it. In a moment, I will look for her, calling her name, stopping strangers and asking, "Have you seen my daughter?" They will think I'm just another exhibit, and maybe I am.

Through the big window, the rain has turned to snow, swirling past the silver buildings. We don't have snow anymore; I don't think Sarah has ever seen it.

Storage and Retrieval

Janet was already three hours delayed when she heard her dead ex-husband being summoned over the courtesy phone at the Atlanta airport. He had left a personal item behind and could claim it at gate D44. Or perhaps she was having auditory hallucinations after three glasses of free Sky Club Chardonnay. But no. There was the announcement again. Her dead ex-husband had left a personal item at gate D44. Well, of course it wasn't him, just someone with the same name: Ronnie Rogers. Like a child in a cowboy movie. The marriage had lasted almost five years, almost two decades ago. By the time he was killed on the motorcycle he'd bought after the divorce, they hadn't spoken in years.

Janet stuffed more popcorn into her mouth. On the barstools to her right, a couple in matching green sweaters was arguing over whether their cat could be safely left with someone named Taffy. To her left, a dreadlocked white guy poked at his phone.

"I wonder what that man left behind at gate D44," she said to him. "What constitutes a personal item? Underpants?"

The man blinked at her. "That would be pretty personal," he said. He had an accent she couldn't quite place.

She was aware of him regarding her with bemusement, the way most people did when they first saw her. She knew she resembled a twelve-year-old with an aging disease: slim preteen body, long auburn hair, and wrinkles. "You're an odd sort of creature, looks-wise," her last boyfriend had told her, just before breaking up with her, which was the same thing he told her just before hooking up with her.

"Where are you going?" she asked the dreadlocked guy. Wine made her nosy. "Where are you from?"

He gave her a steady, annoyed look. He was probably her own age, mid-forties. "I'm from Denver," he said. "I'm going to Denver."

"I'm a librarian," she said. "I'm going to meet a robot." This was true. The man smiled and turned away. She knew nothing about robots, which was why she had to go meet one in person. But would she ever get there? The couple beside her hauled their considerable asses off their stools. "Woohey, drunk," said the woman. The announcement came again: Ronnie Rogers, where could you be? We need you here at gate D44, to claim your underpants, or your monogrammed toothbrush, or your phone with the contacts of all the people you ever loved or tried to love.

The Sky Club was at Gate D27, and her flight from D13 was still delayed. Who was this Ronnie Rogers? Was he anything like her own? Maybe it was nostalgia that gripped her, maybe it was something else. She checked around herself to make sure she'd gathered all of her own personal items. "I'm off," she said to the dreadlocked man. Off my rocker, off my ass, off my axis. He didn't look up. "Going to look for my dead ex-husband."

"Have a good trip," the man said.

•

The robot Janet was going to meet lived in the library of a Midwestern university. As part of her new head librarian duties, she had purchased a similar robot for her own

Georgia university, to be delivered next month. She just needed to learn how to operate the thing. It was a revolutionary way of storing and retrieving. No longer would students waste time browsing gold-embossed spines; no longer would couples, brains a-tingle, fall into scandalous embrace surrounded by musty, lusty volumes of medieval French literature. At least the study carrels could stay. It was the books that were on the way out—or rather, on the way to the library's new climate-controlled wing, where they would be scanned and then stored according to size— size!—in bins stacked like tiny skyscrapers four stories tall.

In a YouTube video, a cheerful voiceover described how the new system stored books and journals in "one ninth the space needed for shelves, making room for more workstations, computers, and study areas." The camera panned over an empty-looking room where multicultural students sat at round tables, smiling stiffly at each other.

The best part of the video was where the robot, a four-story-tall yellow crane that looked like a forklift mated with a dinosaur, raced along a track and pulled out a bookshelf-sized bin—so quick, so easy—and brought it, like a hurrying butler, to the work station where a human being plucked out the correct book to scan and send to the circulation desk. All in ten minutes or less from the time the smiling students clicked their request.

Sometimes, in her dreams, Janet saw the robot moving through her body, retrieving bones and cells and then restoring them, traveling along the track of her spine from her brain to her belly. She saw the robot open a drawer and peer in, then close it and zoom away.

•

She hurried past the Coffee Bean & Tea Leaf, the Atlanta Daily World store, the Delta employees hawking American Express cards, and the people dressed in shorts for the Atlanta September or coats for the wintery place they were headed. She didn't realize she'd been running until she stopped running. D44 was where the terminal terminated in a pod of gate areas and chairs and passengers sitting on the floor glaring at their laptops. Behind the gray-haired man standing at the D44 counter a sign said that Flight 4315 would be departing in an hour for a place Janet had never heard of.

Her own Ronnie had never been on an airplane. They'd met in high school in a bland suburb of Baltimore, Janet Rogers and Ronnie Rogers—how funny would it be if they got married? They'd married when they were nineteen, to their parents' delight, not just because they had the same last name but because she thought she was pregnant. He'd been a tall, laughing boy with thick dark hair, prone to practical jokes that often took a turn for the near-fatal (the wall of fire in the street; the sleeping pills in his mother's martini). He was an Elvis fan, so they'd driven to Memphis for their honeymoon, toured Graceland, and stayed two nights at the Peabody, where they saw the ducks march from their penthouse elevator down a red carpet and plop, plop, plop into the lobby pond.

"Someday," Ronnie had said, squeezing her close, "we're gonna live like those ducks."

She wasn't pregnant after all. She finished her English degree and read novels out loud to Ronnie to help him sleep. He worked at a garage and came home smelling of gasoline and oil and sweat, and she loved him for this, and for his big, loud body and his big, stupid dreams. When she told him she'd been accepted to a master's program in Alabama, he said, "Well, there's no way I'm going to Alabama," but she'd known that already, and known already that he was sleeping with the chirpy cashier at the garage, who smelled of jasmine.

She watched as the gray-haired Delta employee at the gate D44 counter picked up his phone. "Ronnie Rogers," he said solemnly, as if issuing a call to prayer. "Please come to gate D44 to retrieve a personal item."

How long would he keep doing this? At what point did he decide, Fuck it, Ronnie Rogers, your personal item goes to the land of lost personal items, never to be seen again?

And then Janet felt her breath stall in her throat as a tall man in a khaki windbreaker hurried to the counter and said something in a loud, laughing voice. It wasn't exactly Ronnie, not quite; not the Ronnie she knew, but the Ronnie he might have turned into, forty-five years old, a little chubby, a little bald. The man behind the counter nodded and handed over a small orange case. It was shaped like a cube. It had a little handle. Ronnie Rogers took the case and hurried away, back up the corridor toward the D gates and the C gates and the rest of the entire world, and Janet— slightly drunk, yes, and stunned, and delayed forever, it seemed—turned and followed.

•

The week before, she'd had a party at her house to celebrate the purchase of the robot, and her colleagues gathered in Janet's kitchen, eating Triscuits and brie, drinking beers and doing shots of Jägermeister because why the hell not? Janet showed everyone the YouTube videos of the robot doing its thing, and everyone said, *Wow, we were expecting something cuter.*

"Cuter, how?" Janet asked.

"With a personality at least," said her friend Molly. Molly was director of acquisitions and six months away from retirement; she wasn't keen on the idea of having to work with a robot. She'd been the one to catch her own grad assistant stealing books and reported him to Janet, who reported him to the dean, who had him arrested. "Maybe with a little face and little hands."

Janet didn't care that her robot had no face and no hands. It did what it was meant to do; it held the things it was meant to hold. "It ingests the scanned books," she explained. "And then it remembers where they are."

"It doesn't *remember*," Molly protested. "It doesn't *ingest*. I mean, I wish!"

"Well, call it what you want," Janet said, cheerfully. She didn't care what anybody thought. She knew the robot worked the way memories worked. All the big things stored together: a father's death, a first kiss, a penis on the subway. All of this in the same bin. Winning ten bucks at slots, an argument with the Target cashier, a broken basement window: all stored together in smaller bins, just as accessible if that's what you were looking for.

She tried not to let it bother her that there had been a petition, signed by over fifty faculty, protesting the cost of the robot—almost two million dollars—which could have been put, according to them, to better use. What about adjunct salaries? What about the computers that could no longer compute? "They need to suck it up and get with the future," Janet had said to Molly. "The future's so bright, I gotta wear shades. Remember that song?"

Molly smiled miserably and said, "We should get your robot a Twitter account," and Janet felt a swell of gratitude.

•

Ronnie Rogers was a fast walker, but he'd always been a fast walker. He had the orange cube case gripped in his left hand, because even back from the dead he was still left-handed. Or not from the dead: he'd faked his death, obviously. "Ha," Janet said out loud, dodging a beeping cart bearing an elderly couple. He'd been big on practical jokes. He'd liked movies with twists at the end. Faking one's death did seem like a strange thing to do, but—as Janet liked to say—it took a lot to surprise her these days. Nothing seemed entirely out of the realm of possibility. Last summer, they'd had a problem with students making a racket in the library as they tried to catch invisible monsters with their phones. And last spring, there had been an active shooter alert, and Janet, Molly, and three students spent an hour crouched in the locked technology classroom waiting to die. The text messages brought news of carnage. One shooter, then two. Seven dead in the library; cafeteria workers shot in the dish room. So specific. Then it turned out there wasn't a shooter at all; it was a false alarm. All clear. All fake. What could you make of a world where two things were true at the same time? For instance: Ronnie was dead. But also, Ronnie was alive, and striding very quickly through the Atlanta airport.

She joined the surge of people heading for the escalators that led down to the plane train, finding herself lodged behind a large family with a stroller. She could just make out the glow of Ronnie's now-bald head far below. He looked as if he'd forgotten to apply sunscreen, like maybe he'd spent the summer—doing what? Boating? They'd gone boating once, in Annapolis. They'd eaten ham sandwiches, and they drank lukewarm wine on a blanket on a hill and had sex in the crabgrass.

That was a bin she wasn't expecting to open, but *voilà*, there it was.

She pushed her way down the escalator, her rolling bag thwumping behind her. "The plane train is now approaching," said a friendly female automated voice. She sounded like a gentle robot, like she might have a little face and hands. The plane train slid to a stop; the doors heaved open, the crowd surged; a teddy bear backpack struck her softly in the chin. Janet could see Ronnie up ahead. He boarded. She boarded, one car behind, moved to the front to stare at him through the glass. What if he looked up and saw her? She moved behind a tall woman with spikey red hair. But he wasn't looking.

It occurred to her that even though she could remember the itch of crabgrass on her thighs, she couldn't remember if his obituary had mentioned children. Wait: had she actually seen his obituary? And now that she was thinking about it, why was it that she'd thought he was dead? Yes: it was one Christmas when her mother said, while slicing

carrots for a stew, "Too bad about Ronnie. Motorcycle accident." But Janet had been involved with Evil Vernon, who
was taking up all the space in her brain. She'd felt a small
pang. But really, a sense of relief, closure. So he was dead:
you couldn't get much more closed than that.

The train was stopping at the C gates. "C for Charlie,"
the female voice said helpfully. In the car up ahead, Ronnie
was staring down at his phone. It was starting to seem as if
perhaps he wasn't just not-dead, but had never been dead;
had been, for the past twenty years, doing whatever it was
he did, living where he lived.

Would he recognize her, with the same hair and body
but a different, older face, the kind of face that would make
more sense if she were more woman-sized, not wearing a
training bra from Walmart? She'd more than once turned
around and startled a teenage boy who'd been following
her. Today, she was wearing her baggy sweater and leg-
gings, which she would swap when she landed for the
pantsuit folded neatly in her bag.

The train slid into B for Bravo. She watched him
through the glass. He stayed where he was, so she stayed
where she was.

There had been fights. He called the cops on her, then
she called the cops on him. She threw his clothes out the
window into the rain. Once, she sliced one wrist with a ser-
rated kitchen knife, and he found her crying and bleeding
under the covers, carried her into the bathroom and ran
the tub full of warm water. He gently removed her clothes,
bandaged and washed her, dried her, tucked her towel-
swaddled back into the bed. This was before the jasmine-
smelling woman. This was just their life together.

File under Adultery. File under Divorce. File under
Gave it a Good Try. After she'd been in Alabama for a couple of weeks, he showed up on her doorstep. It was almost
midnight. "Just let me in," he shouted through the door.
And she shouted back: "No."

When she'd heard he was dead (*had* her mother actually said "dead"?), she'd thought: *There's nothing to apologize for now.*

The train hurtled into the station for A gates, "A for Alpha," and as it slid to a stop she felt her phone buzzing deep in her purse: a text message from the librarian who was picking her up, saying he would meet her in baggage claim. *Looks like your plane is taking off, finally!*

It was?

The doors slid open. She stepped out of the train, around a wheelchair, a schnauzer, a troop of Girl Scouts in their green sashes. And watched Ronnie disappear into the crowd surging toward the escalators.

•

The grad student had managed to steal hundreds of books before Molly caught him. He would fill his backpack with them, cart them home, and sell them on eBay: medieval French literature, physics books from the 1950s, Russian textiles and Finnish fairy tales, a history of the Canadian education system, windmills, codfish, candle-making. Molly had sobbed when she saw his mugshot in the local paper, then said, "Well, that's less to scan anyway," and wiped her eyes. Some of the books had been rescued, but others were out there in the world, with their musty smells and their hard bindings and their pencil-marked notes from long-ago students. Gone forever, but yes—there was less to scan. Less to shelve, less to pile into bins according to size. She felt about those books the same way she felt about Ronnie: something to be retrieved and re-shelved. But which shelf?

At the top of the escalator at the intersection of the A gate corridors, Janet paused in the crowd flowing around her. Ronnie could be in the CNBC News Store, or the Boar's Head, or P. F. Chang's; he could have headed in the direction of A33 or toward A1. A group of backpacking teenagers strode past, laughing. Families with tiny children on leashes. A blind couple with canes stood side-by-side, the man with his hand on the woman's shoulder, while a woman in a Delta uniform stood next to them, talking into a walkie-talkie.

It occurred to her that she could have Ronnie paged: you've left another personal item behind. And then she heard herself being summoned: "Janet Rogers. This is a courtesy warning. Please report to gate D13. Your plane is departing." And she realized she hoped Ronnie didn't hear it; she hoped he was enjoying being not-dead, chatting on the phone with his wife, or browsing through a magazine, or doing anything at all but opening up that tiny drawer that held the contents of their life together. The blind couple headed off down the corridor, their arms linked; more backpackers streamed past. Her name came again, one last warning, one last courtesy, before the plane took off and left her behind.

Acknowledgments

I am grateful to the editors and staff of the following journals where these stories first appeared, sometimes in slightly different form:

"Perishables" appeared in *Post Road*
"Witnesses" in *Ninth Letter*
"Seven Ravens" in *Blackbird*
"The Age of Discovery" in *The Southampton Review*
"The Celebrity" in *Memorious*
"Young Susan" in *Cream City Review*
"Hi Ho Cherry-O" in *Witness* and *Pushcart Prize XLIV*
"Sea Ice" in *The Journal*
"Sharon by the Seashore" in *Ploughshares*
"Cornfield, Cornfield, Cornfield" in *Wigleaf*
"Rise" in *New England Review*
"Hematite, Apatite" in *Shenandoah*
"Fillies" in *Washington Square Review*
"Basic Commands" in *Southern Humanities Review*
"The Sitters" in *Confrontation*
"Starry Night" in *The Gettysburg Review*
"In the Museum of Tense Moments" in *The Greensboro Review*
"Storage and Retrieval" in *The Oxford American*

My thanks to Tracie Stewart, Shalyn Claggett, Holly Johnson, Mike Kardos, Katie Pierce, Kelly Marsh, Mike Rice, Emily Stinson, Joyce McMahon, Cathleen Keenan, Lynda Majarian, Danielle Carter. I am grateful to the Department of English at Mississippi State, and to my colleagues and students. Thanks also to Michelle Herman, *The Journal*, and to everyone at The Ohio State University Press and Mad Creek Books. Thanks to my husband, Troy DeRego, the best person I can think of to both travel the world with and be stuck at home with; and to my sister, Cindy Perdue; my mom, Carolyn Fisher; and my in-laws, Rod and Elaine DeRego.

And to my dad, Richard Hagenston, one of the best story tellers I know: This book is dedicated to you.

THE JOURNAL NON/FICTION PRIZE
(formerly The Ohio State University Prize in Short Fiction)

The Age of Discovery and Other Stories
BECKY HAGENSTON

Sign Here If You Exist and Other Essays
JILL SISSON QUINN

When: Stories
KATHERINE ZLABEK

Out of Step: A Memoir
ANTHONY MOLL

Brief Interviews with the Romantic Past
KATHRYN NUERNBERGER

Landfall: A Ring of Stories
JULIE HENSLEY

Hibernate
ELIZABETH ESLAMI

The Deer in the Mirror
CARY HOLLADAY

How
GEOFF WYSS

Little America
DIANE SIMMONS

The Book of Right and Wrong
MATT DEBENHAM

The Departure Lounge: Stories and a Novella
PAUL EGGERS

True Kin
RIC JAHNA

Owner's Manual
MORGAN McDERMOTT

Mexico Is Missing: And Other Stories
J. DAVID STEVENS

Ordination
SCOTT A. KAUKONEN

Little Men: Novellas and Stories
GERALD SHAPIRO

The Bones of Garbo
TRUDY LEWIS

The White Tattoo: A Collection of Short Stories
WILLIAM J. COBB

Come Back Irish
WENDY RAWLINGS

Throwing Knives
MOLLY BEST TINSLEY

Dating Miss Universe: Nine Stories
STEVEN POLANSKY

Radiance: Ten Stories
JOHN J. CLAYTON